Reviews

Through this novel, the author
and news reports have all too c
real, devastating impact of the uncertainty into which the
lives of so many EU citizens have been thrown. Beth's
struggles serve as a sobering reminder of how the Brexit
debate has alienated so many members of our community;
that despite their invaluable contribution to all aspects of
society, the events of the past three years have left these
community heroes feeling ostracised. This is a novel that
should be read by all who seek to understand the human
impact of this divisive debate.

Ben Lake MP, Ceredigion

EMJ Foster's writing has summed up the often angst ridden
atmosphere that pervades the whole discourse of the topic of
how Brexit has affected society in Wales. Frequently buried,
but also simmering below the surface, the consequences have
a human scale. Summed up in one sentence: The
protagonist's husband wants her to shut up about them and
accept that it is the way it is and she must simply get on with
her life the way she always has. She feels cracks in more than
her confidence.

The book displays empathy for people and a feeling for how
such a febrile political debate has consequence for real
people.

Mark Strong, Ceredigion Councillor

EMJ Foster's searing polemic tears into hidden and overt racism exposed by the Brexit referendum and sets out the anger, fear, frustration and sense of betrayal of EU citizens who made Britain their home and now feel themselves outcasts. A timely call to arms in the face of a still unfolding serious assault on human rights perpetrated by political forces content to trample on blameless lives.

The book has clever plot-lines with their insightful observations on human relationships which reveal the devastating human repercussions of misunderstandings. The book's dialogue is very authentic. In this book all these things of course are caused by power-struggles of remote political élites, which themselves are to a significant degree subject to the manipulations of other groupings motivated by their own financial and power agendas.

This book is partly about the insidious invasiveness of far-flung lives by these influences. In connection with that, it encompasses a warning to people to be keenly aware that, while such forces need to be challenged, they should be sufficiently circumspect to leave themselves the time and energy to be conscious of the danger of a distortion of reasoning arising from an over-deep immersion in resistance to those forces. Essential reading.

Patrick O'Brien, Journalist

Brexit has preoccupied the lives of us all for the last three years or more, and EMJ Foster's book gives us an all too often unheard voice, the EU national living here in Wales. It tells us of the trials, tribulations of Beth, a feisty university lecturer and Lib Dem Councillor from Belgium who had settled here with Welsh farmer Gavin. As Britain votes for Brexit, her world crumbles and new post referendum insecurities overwhelm her and her marriage. Drawing on many of her own emotions the author portrays Beth as an empathetic, emotional, principled and yet vulnerable individual, who feels let down by all around her. Conventional notions of home evaporate.

For those of us who have held elected public office in recent years much of the story rings true, not least the immense pressure. But few have had their security, stability and predictability of life undermined as EU nationals in the UK.

A fascinating read which reminded me of many issues, and personalities when I was Ceredigion's MP, but one which taught me a lot about the views of EU nationals living in the UK.

Mark Williams, Ceredigion MP 2005-2017

About the Author

EMJ Foster was just 20 years old when she moved to the UK from The Netherlands in 1975. Now married to her second husband, they live a largely self-sufficient lifestyle on the west Wales coast, near Aberaeron, in Ceredigion.

With a degree in Social Policy and Administration, she works as a private tutor in English, Maths and Science, still speaks fluent Dutch and maintains strong links to The Netherlands with a lot of family there.

She has three grown-up children and four grandchildren, enjoys the 'good life', adores long walks and is an avid ballroom dancer.

"I have been a campaigner on environmental and social issues since I can remember thinking for myself. Through writing I can express my frustrations, highlight injustices and, hopefully, offer solutions.

Besides novels, I have written a few plays, short stories and a number of poems,"

E M J Foster

I dedicate this book
to the 3.6 million EU Citizens
who have made the UK their home,
who have contributed so much of their energy
to making the UK a wonderful, diverse nation;
who have enriched the lives of many and
who deserve praise for their forbearance.

Acknowledgements

I wish to thank the following people.

First of all my family, my husband, children and grandchildren, for standing by me in my moments of despair when I really struggled to know where my home is. My friends too who have anchored me.

Next I wish to thank Ceredigion County Council for voting unanimously to ask the UK Government to scrap the 'settled status' scheme, for their unstinting support for EU Citizens, their understanding and appreciation of people like me.

A very profound thank you is due to Lorraine Hills for reading my original manuscript and detailing improvements. Also, for being a wonderful friend.

Finally, I wish to thank Karen Gemma Brewer, my publisher, for having faith in me.

Preface

Home?
What is it?
Where is it?

"I feel so utterly unwanted."

"How can you say that, you of all people, involved in everything!"

"That doesn't mean I'm wanted!"

"You must ignore what some people say."

"Easy for you to say; you're not the foreigner!"

"I don't see you as a foreigner."

"No, but the Government does and people who hate foreigners do!"

Chapter 1 – Conscientious

The phone rings. It breaks into the embarrassed silence. Visual relief shows on Beth's face. "Hello?" She listens intently for a minute. "Ok, I'll be there in two minutes."

She quietly puts her mobile in her pocket, picks up her glasses and puts her coat on. Gavin looks at her expectantly. "It's Anna, she's had an accident. She needs me!" Beth is glad to get away from her argument with Gavin. She absolutely hates arguing but Gavin is being so blunt with her, so uncaring, not understanding a word she's saying. She's fed up with going over the same points again and again. She hates the silences too, that follow. It's her only weapon though. He hates it more than she does.

Beth walks out of the back door, down the lane and crosses the main road. She lets herself in by the back door of a bungalow. Her elderly neighbour is sitting on the sofa, her phone next to her.

"Thank you so much for coming straightaway. I don't like to be a bother."

"Don't worry Anna," Beth interrupts, "You know you can always phone me, it's no bother. Now, what have you done?"

"I was cleaning the top cupboards in the kitchen and, I don't know, I must've missed the step. The next thing I'm on the floor. I've tried phoning Mared but she must be at work."

"Where have you hurt yourself?"

"My leg hurts and my left arm."

"Let's have a look." Beth examines Anna carefully. "I think you need to have both of them x-rayed. Have you got Mared's mobile? I'll text her and then I'll phone for an ambulance."

"I don't want to go to hospital."

"Sweetheart, you have no option, but it may not be broken. I'm sure you'll be straight home."

"But who will feed the animals?"

"I'll ask Gavin to look after them today. Now, where's your phonebook?"

That evening Gavin's in a foul mood. "What you go offering my services for? Can't her own kids ever do anything for her? Why did you have to volunteer me?"

"Oh, stop whinging, will you. It's only likely to be for a few days. We'll manage. We always do."

Gavin slams the door as he leaves the house. Beth groans, "Bloody typical! Never prepared to put himself out for anybody else! Typical, typical!" Her voice becomes high-pitched and screechy. She's crying tears of frustration. She wipes them away quickly as she notices Mared in the hall, knocking tentatively on the kitchen door.

"Sorry, I didn't think you'd mind; I've let myself in."

Beth cringes but forces a smile. "Don't worry, come in, you want a cuppa?"

"Thanks, no, I just came to give you an update on Mam."

"Yeh, of course, sit down. Has she had the x-rays?"

"Yes, her leg is not broken, just badly bruised, but she has broken her wrist. They're keeping her in overnight and will put it in plaster tomorrow. I'm bringing her home in the afternoon."

"She won't be able to do much I take it. Who's going to look after her?"

"You know what Mam's like, independent, and she hates strangers in her home." Mared hesitates. Beth looks her straight in the eye. "I was hoping you might pop in on a daily basis and maybe Gavin will take care of the pigs. I, I am away with work next week and....."

"You will have to ask Gavin yourself. As for me popping in, that's not a problem. I can pop in in the mornings and early evenings. However, I am away myself in a few weeks, just for a week back to Belgium. You can't ask Gavin to help your mother with dressing or things like that. How about Huw? Can he help out at all?"

"I've not spoken to him yet; he's not answering his phone."

"Would you like to use my phone? He really ought to know. Are you sure you haven't got time for a cup of tea?"

"No really, I need to pack Mam's bag and go back to the hospital. I'll try Huw again when I'm there."

"Ok then, I'll see you tomorrow when you bring your mum back. Do look out for Gavin. He should be with your mum's pigs soon. He's just seeing to the cows first."

"I'm not really dressed for the pigsty." Mared looks down at her high heels and her designer dress. Her face shows disgust at the thought of the pigsty.

"There's an overall and your mum's wellies in the shed. Sure she won't mind you borrowing them."

"I'm not sure. Can't you ask Gavin for me?" Mared puts on her most pathetic face, large eyes, simpering smile. It's what Beth dislikes most about Mared. She may have a grand well-paid job in the media but she uses weak feminine wiles at the

12

mere hint of a bit of muck or a spider.

"I can't ask Gavin as he has his own timetable, his own jobs."

"Ok, I'll look out for him. I'd better go." Mared looks disappointed as she leaves.

Beth watches her through the window. Mared carefully places her feet in patches of the lane that have no water or mud. "Stuck up cow. She probably heard me when she came in. See if I care!" Beth is wiping away more tears as she says this, knowing her normal confidence has cracked. It's been like this the whole month, following the Referendum result. She and Gavin have been arguing ever since. Beth has cried buckets whilst Gavin appears completely relaxed about leaving the EU. The more Beth weeps, the more impatient he is. He understands her feelings but wants her to shut up about them and accept that it is the way it is and she must simply get on with her life the way she always has. She feels cracks in more than her confidence. She feels unbalanced, unhinged, unreal, the ground has been removed from underneath her and Gavin is not holding her hand to make sure she doesn't fall.

She'll be there for Anna, no doubt, but something is nagging at her usual willingness. She feels used; it's a new feeling. Gavin's reluctance to help is amplifying this sense. Mared asking him is more likely to produce the desired result. He'll probably be all sweetness and smiles, she thinks.

Chapter 2 – Doubting

"I've got to go to market tomorrow. Beth, are you taking any notice of what I'm saying?"

"I heard you. So, you've got the market, so what?" Beth carries on looking at her phone.

"I can't do Anna's animals. I just can't fit it in. I'm bloody knackered. I've been at it now for over a month."

"It's been just three weeks."

"Well, it feels like a bloody month. Anyway, I'm not doing them tomorrow." Gavin picks up his porridge bowl and digs his spoon in it aggressively.

"If you can't manage Anna's pigs tomorrow, why don't you phone Huw and get him to do them? I would offer to help more but James Coburn has just emailed me to say he can see me tomorrow." Beth looks up.

"About bloody time too!"

"I don't know why you're so cross, it's not as if you've tried to do something to help me. I always have to do these kinds of things myself. You haven't stuck up for me one little bit; you haven't been to any public meetings, street stalls ….."

"Change the record. You know you're good at that kind of stuff. Do we have to go over this, two months after the bloody Referendum?"

"Here we go again, poor old Gavin, Mister Uneducated, who can't do these kinds of things, his wife has to do it all by herself yet again!" She hears her own voice in her head telling her to shut up. "Anyway, tomorrow I'm off to town to see James Coburn but I'll see to Anna before I go, I'll water the seedlings here, sort out the emails, feed the chickens and the geese and I'll do the shopping whilst I'm in town. Thought I might pop into the Uni too, sort out my office."

"Why don't you go to the prom and do a stand-up whilst you're there!"

"Very funny, sarky!"

"I'm off!" Gavin shoves his bowl in the sink.

"You think you might at least rinse your bowl! Are you going to phone Huw or what?"

"I'll do it later. Leave the washing up." Gavin brushes his lips past her head in a gesture of affection and grabs the dog lead.

Beth sighs when he's gone. "What am I going to do? I absolutely hate all this!" She turns on her computer and types in her password in a total trance. She pours herself a coffee and sits in front of the screen. She has at least 20 emails to answer or delete. She opens the one from James Coburn and replies:

> "Dear James, Thank you very much for all you're doing to help me. I shall accept your kind offer to see me tomorrow, 11 August, at 10.30.
> Best wishes, Beth."

She races through the new emails, deletes what she can, answers the rest curtly and makes notes on her pad to deal with them later. She quickly scans her Facebook messages and looks at her new campaign page. "Three new members, lovely, well, hope they're lovely in any case." Satisfied, she turns off the computer, gulps her coffee and gets up. "Right, chickens, geese, pick the salad leaves, hang out the washing, pop in and see Anna, off to the Council. Have I got my papers, purse, phone, pen, pad, my five p's?"

Anna is pleased to see her. She has managed to dress herself and has made her own breakfast.

"Guess what, I'm seeing James Coburn tomorrow."

"Well, that's good news I suppose." The way Anna speaks, Beth's not sure if she's sincere. "Don't worry about me anymore. In fact, I'll be ok except for the pigs."

"You sure?"

"You've done plenty for me already. And Mared can take me shopping at the weekends."

"Has Huw been to see you this week?"

"No, but he has phoned, that's something."

"It's just that," Beth hesitates.

"What Beth?"

"Oh nothing, Gavin will sort it. Well, I must go. The Council meeting starts in half an hour. I'll pop in at the end of the week but, please, please, phone me if you need me before." She hugs Anna who gives her a warm appreciative smile.

She closes the door, leaving Anna in her own loneliness. Beth's shoulders sink visibly. One burden less she thinks and hates herself for it, but she can't help it. She has noticed this feeling of discomfort in Anna's behaviour whenever she talks about her own problems. For the moment she decides to shrug it off. She starts the car and heads for the Council meeting.

Chapter 3 – Relieved

The alarm goes off at five. Beth struggles to turn it off and bring herself to her senses. Her back is stiff, her brain in a fuzz. Gavin hasn't heard the alarm and is sleeping quietly next to her. She stretches her legs, turns carefully onto her other side and slips out of bed. She reaches for her dressing gown and gently opens the bedroom door. First a cup of tea, then a shower, then the emails, then breakfast, then tea for Gavin, no, first tea, then the emails, then the pigs, geese, then shower, then tea for Gavin. She sorts her list of jobs whilst negotiating the stairs. She takes the steps like a toddler so as to remain quiet. She makes a cup of tea and cuddles herself on the sofa. She could so easily go back to sleep. "Bloody Gavin, why couldn't he get up a bit earlier? If we all did a bit more, then people like me wouldn't have to do a whole lot extra. I sound just like my mother."

Beth is feeling bitter and in such a mood she still mutters to herself out loud. "Anna's pigs won't get fed because she can't do it. Neither Huw, nor Mared, nor Gavin will do it, so that leaves me, real world people like me. They say they will do this and that and then leave it to me! Yes! This is the real world!"

She turns her computer on. Nothing much has happened since she checked her emails last night except a distant nephew showing off more of his biceps.

Outside a weak sun is trying to rise above the trees, matching Beth's mood. She puts on her overalls over her dressing gown, shivers as she puts her bare feet into her wellies and opens the back door. The fresh air has a reviving effect upon Beth. She lets the chickens and geese out, waters the seedlings, squashes a host of slugs and goes across the road to see to Anna's pigs.

The road is desirably deserted. "Wish it could stay like this, just me on this planet, no demands on me, the whole planet for me, I'd be welcome in every corner, on every continent. I wouldn't feel an alien." The pigs have heard her and smelled her tea breath. They start to grunt and shove. She opens the sty and strokes the first one. "Shh, Spotty, don't wake Anna. Come on, let's find you some pignuts."

Spotty squeals in anticipation. Beth quickly fills the buckets. The pigs slurp noisily while Beth fetches fresh water and opens the gates.

It's nearly six o'clock as she almost runs back across the road; she has reordered her jobs and wishes to surprise Gavin with a cup of tea before she heads for the shower. Her brain is constantly changing things round, seeing things in different ways. It has been running away with her emotions. She is desperately sorting out the muddle that has been plaguing her for the past few weeks. Once in the house, she changes her mind again. In her living room she opens her laptop and types away furiously. All her pent-up anger and frustration flow into an angry letter to the local press. The feeling of relief is overwhelming.

Chapter 4 – Principled

The door opens. James Coburn's secretary lets Beth in. "Take a seat. He won't be long." Jill gets back behind her computer and ignores Beth.

Beth opens her briefcase, takes out the letter she has sent to Theresa May, puts her glasses on, searches for a pen, takes a gulp of water from her bottle, puts her car keys in her pocket, anything to keep her busy; Beth can't cope with sitting still and doing nothing except stare into space. Meditation's not her style. Her thoughts are in a whirl; no calming voices spring forward. She tries to replay in her head the scene at six that morning when she'd brought Gavin a cup of tea in bed and announced she'd already dealt with Anna's pigs. For the second time this week Gavin's angry words mingle with her own defensive ones, her resentment feels as if it is going to balloon out of her head. Gavin's sarcastic, cutting tone slices the resentment balloon in half. It doesn't pop, it doesn't shrivel up; it grows bigger and turns red, angry red.

James Coburn's jolly voice forces Beth to close the lid on her private personal problems, focus on her public personal problems, dredge up a smile, her inane grin, become Miss Capable, Miss Potent, Miss Not-to-be-messed-with!

James Coburn shakes hands with a young couple, promises to be in touch as soon as possible and turns his head in Beth's direction. "Come in Beth," he welcomes with a warm smile. "Jill, can you bring in a print-out of Beth's letter?"

"I've got a copy here," Beth interjects.

"Efficient as always. Ok, Jill, don't worry." James Coburn closes the door, sits down and reads Beth's letter through.

"Fantastic letter, you've said it all. You've still not had a reply?"

"I have, here's a copy. It's typical, a standard response."

It takes James Coburn 20 seconds to scan Theresa May's reply, while Beth scans his face.

"Ok, I will write to Theresa May myself and to the Home Office. I totally agree that you can't stay in this limbo situation. You deserve better than this."

"It's not just me though, I'm not campaigning just for myself; there are three million of us, three million in my situation, three million of us being used as bargaining chips."

"They won't have all been here as long as you though."

"So what, do you think it's ok to send some of us back, what, let's say, those who have been here less than five years, two years, ten years?" Beth's inner voice is urging her to stay calm.

James Coburn hesitates. "The country has voted Brexit and the Prime Minister has vowed she will honour that. She has to make some concessions to the Brexiteers." His voice is soft and gentle and his face is sincere.

"I thought you were with us, you stood next to me at every street stall, you argued what I argued, you, you..." Beth's private personal problems are invading her public personal ones. The red balloon is threatening to burst behind her eyeballs. She gropes for a hankie and dabs her eyes, blows her nose. It's no good; the pressure is too great. "Sorry, sorry about that. It's all been so exhausting."

"Don't be sorry Beth. I've never met someone as caring as you. I do," James Coburn speaks haltingly, picking his words carefully. "I do agree with you but we've been forced into a difficult position."

"You mean your constituency is a marginal one and you're worried, or the Conservatives, your party bosses, have told you what to say or UKIP might unseat you." Beth sounds bitter.

"It's called pragmatism."

"Pragmatism over principle."

"C'mon Beth, you Lib Dems know a thing or two about that."

"Yes, but not me." Beth has managed to deflate the red balloon and puts her hankie away. "Anyway, what do you propose to write?" She suddenly sounds as if she couldn't care less.

James Coburn looks at her slightly surprised. "I'll make the point that for those EU nationals living here who have made the UK their home and have contributed so wonderfully, that they deserve an answer soon, that they shouldn't be used as bargaining chips and, if you're ok with it, I'll use you as an exemplary model citizen who deserves to have her questions answered. Are you ok with that?"

"Fine, thank you."

Beth has sunk into a controlled despair mode. To the outside world, to James Coburn, to Jill, she looks like Dr Beth Evans, Lecturer in Planning, Cllr Beth Evans, Liberal Democrat Party stalwart, Beth Evans, wife to Gavin, local farmer, Beth, Belgian by birth but welcomed in the UK for over three decades, the woman everybody asks to join their committees because you always ask the busiest person and Beth is a busy person. To her inside, the world that only Beth inhabits, the world that Gavin only glimpses on occasions, she is just Beth, lonely Beth who feels abandoned by everybody else, Beth who has started to question her own identity, Beth who doesn't feel welcome in the UK any more, Beth who doesn't feel that Belgium is home either, not after 30 years, Beth who is so confused she can't untangle private from public at certain moments, for whom all is problem, problem.

She wants to scream but she gets up, smiles, shakes James Coburn by the hand and walks out of his office. Tory traitor, snake in the grass! These are the words that echo in her head.

"I'll be in touch with you as soon as I have an answer." James Coburn puts on his professional smirk.

Jill lets Beth out. "Bye Beth."

"Bye."

Beth walks over to her car; she holds her head high. From the window James Coburn, if he were looking, can only see the slim figure confidently getting the car keys out and sliding delicately behind the wheel. Nobody notices Beth's face with the tears streaming down her cheeks. Nobody hears her loud mutterings, her despairing language, her primitive outpourings, her red balloon bursting.

Beth puts off her Uni work and goes home.

"Are you still in a bad mood with me?"

"I'm beyond bad moods; I'm beyond, beyond every mood. I just feel numb."

"All because I was cross with you this morning! Look, I'm sorry, you just surprised me so early. You just make me feel so useless sometimes."

"It's ok Gavin, you and me rowing is nothing compared to how I feel today."

"Do you want a cup of tea? Why don't you run a bath and relax? I'll bring the tea up. Then you can tell me all about it."

Gavin at his best. Gavin at his most loving, the Gavin she met 25 years ago at Reading Festival, Gavin with the same cheeky grin who knows how to make her feel better. Beth drops her stuff in the study and walks upstairs to the bedroom. She runs the bath and strips. She looks at herself in the mirror. She can't judge whether she looks good for 50. She's still slim but then, she's never had any children in her womb. Her hair is thick and easy to manage; she has it professionally cut every month. She doesn't go to the gym; it's enough for her to do her garden and the chickens and geese plus all the farm work

Gavin needs help with.

Gavin walks in with the tea. He looks at Beth looking in the mirror. They catch each other's eyes. Gavin puts the cup down, comes over and puts an arm around her. "You're as beautiful now as you were when I met you."

"Yeh, right, and your eyesight has definitely deteriorated."

"Excuse me, I still have 20-20 vision."

"Well, you haven't seen these dark patches under my eyes nor my arms sagging, nor….."

"Well, at least it isn't your tits." Gavin takes both her nipples in his hands, turns her round and kisses them in turn. Beth lets out a soft moan. Yes, Gavin knows all her weak spots.

Their lovemaking is quick and noisy. Her tea is still hot when she sits on the edge of the bed afterwards and the bath is not overflowing. She's relieved to sink under the bubbles.

A gorgeous smell wafts upstairs. Gavin is roasting lamb, her favourite meal. Beth climbs out of the bath and puts on a simple T-shirt and jeans. She ruffles her hair and descends into the aroma of rosemary and garlic. The table is laid, a glass of wine is waiting. She doesn't want to burst this bubble of bliss with her tales of anti-foreigner woe. Neither does she want to bottle it up any longer. Her skin feels soft, her hair clean, her love for Gavin at this moment is strong but her mind is muddled.

"Go on, sit down, enjoy the wine. Dinner is going to be at

least another half hour. So, what happened today?"

"My meeting with James Coburn, you mean? Total waste of time! He's done sod all and that's a fact. For such a prominent Pro-Remainer to have changed, he's a, he's a, he's a bloody traitor!" There, she has said it now and with it she bursts into tears. "He might as well have been on the Brexit side," she sobs. "He's just totally changed his tune." Her voice is cracking and pitching at the same time. "And you know what the worst of it is?"

"Go on!"

"He expects me, me," she jabs hard at herself, "me to be the understanding one, me, the European Migrant, I am supposed to suddenly be anti-myself now!" Beth blows her nose in one of Gavin's large hankies and gulps half her glass of wine.

"Steady on Beth! So what did James Coburn actually say he's going to do?"

"Oh, he'll write a letter on my behalf but not on behalf of European Migrants as a whole. I should be ok, but people like Sophia, well, he probably thinks she should bugger off!"

Chapter 5 – Concerned

Beth's office is her sanctuary. She has a large window that looks out over the sea. The door has a window to the corridor. Her office is fortunately at the end so not many people ogle in. She drops her bag, turns on her computer and makes herself a coffee. She stares out of the window. The seascape is the same today as last week and the week before that. She can't swear it is the same as when she was given this post 20 years ago. Gradual changes, new buildings, different advertising hoardings, renewed sea defences, she knows they've occurred but she can't picture the seascape beyond a few weeks ago.

She watches the people on the beach. They're too far away to see details, to see what colour the individuals are, to see what items of clothing they're wearing.

Her brain can't focus even after coffee. She knows she came to tidy but she feels like packing it all up. She has felt like that ever since her visit to James Coburn the previous week. Even her few days away to see her mum in Belgium hasn't lifted her spirits.

A knock on her door forces her face into Ms Professional. "Come in!" She turns and the smile that appears is genuine. "Hi Sophia, you're back early!"

"I've managed to get a summer job so I never went home." Sophia's words come out clear but it's clear too from her accent that she's not British.

"What's the summer job?"

"Waitressing in that new four star hotel on the seafront and looking after the front desk as well as a bit of bedroom cleaning at times. There are a few other Romanian girls so it's been ok. Well, it was ok." The last four words are said so low under Sophia's breath, Beth doesn't hear them.

"Are they students too?"

"No, they're here with an agent, just to work in hotels."

"Anyway, it must be lovely to speak your own language with these girls. But what can I do for you today? We don't start back for another couple of weeks."

"I know. I read the article in the Herald today and thought I'd see you. So I asked the secretary to let me know when you get in."

"You could've emailed me."

"I know but I didn't have the words to describe what I have to tell you." Sophia's eye's lower, her face looks pained and Beth feels her pulse begin to thump in her head.

"Do you want a coffee Sophia? Come and sit down."

Sophia sits on the edge of the proffered chair but declines the coffee. She looks uncomfortable as she tells her story. She frequently stops whilst searching for the appropriate words in English. After two years as a student in the UK, her English is fantastic; she can write almost word perfect essays on the flaws of the British planning system. Her hesitations are a sign of her distress, a sign of having to find words for experiences beyond her understanding.

Beth is patient. She can recall exactly what she wrote in the Herald last week. She had altered her early morning's creation in a temper after her visit to James Coburn. She had not been very careful with her words; she had felt very emotional. She had wanted to call all Brexiteers bigots and racists and bastards but had managed to insert the words many and some for all, and changed bastards to buffoons.

Beth realises that even after that bit of editing, her article had not been written in the most diplomatic of language. She feels a twinge of shame but her anger at Brexit and her disappointment in James Coburn's lame behaviour soon drowns that emotion.

Sophia is in tears by the time she has finished. Beth hands her a tissue. "I'm so sorry you have had to endure this abuse. Are you intending to stay working in this hotel or will you find another term-time job? Do you need a job at all for your final year?"

"I'm not sure I want to stay for a third year."

"Don't say that! You're one of my best students! You can't give up as a result of a few, a few bigoted losers; yes, losers. They're losers and you're a winner; you're bright and...."

Sophia interrupts: "Thank you Beth for your kind words but the Remain campaigners lost the vote and that lot didn't." Her face contorts back into itself. "You didn't see their nasty faces."

"We should go to the police. Were they drunk?"

"They were the next day but not when they first attacked us. I did complain to the boss but he said we should just put up with it, said it's just 'banter', sorry, I don't know that word. He did send this bloke from the kitchen up with us girls the next morning to help clear the rooms."

"So the boss realised you may need some protection. What's his name? I did read about him in the Herald when he opened the Glan-y-Môr."

"He's Peter Mezzo, of Italian origin, well, his great-grandfather was Italian. His family made lots of money selling ice-cream."

"Of course! I haven't had the chance to meet him personally. The Glan-y-Môr is not in my ward. By the way, banter means words said for a bit of fun, harmless. Well, what you experienced is not banter; it's harassment, sexual harassment and it's racist abuse."

"You should have seen the state of the rooms the next morning. They smelled of urine and alcohol. I took some photographs on my mobile. It's against policy of the hotel but I don't care." Sophia gets out her smartphone and quickly finds the file she's looking for. Beth squats next to her. "That one I took in the bathroom. They wrote that with lipstick on the mirror. And that one I took in another bedroom. The writing is on the dressing table mirror."

Beth is shocked. "What did you do when you saw the state of these rooms? What did the other girls do? And what about the chap?" She knows she's rambling but feels suddenly overwhelmed with this latest knowledge of hate crime.

"The bloke from the kitchen is Hungarian. His English is ok but not good enough for arguing with the boss. I went down to have a word him, with the boss that is. He was in the dining room with this group of 'stag-men', is that what you call them? Well, he was laughing and joking with them. He spotted me and came over to the doorway. I explained the state of the rooms and asked if he'd like to see them. He said, 'We can't afford bad publicity, we need all the customers we can get so just clear it all up and stop making such a fuss, will you!' He then walked back and apologised to them. They saw the whole thing."

"I think I need to go and have a word with this Peter Mezzo." Beth is totally indignant.

"I wouldn't if I were you Beth."

"Why not? We don't allow racist abuse in this neck of the woods."

"Neck of the woods?"

"Sorry Sophia, it's something we say. We mean this part of the country. It was a stupid term to use in any case. We don't allow racist abuse anywhere in this country!"

"I still don't think you should go and see this man. I've done some detective work since that, that awful weekend."

"Have there been any more incidents?"

"No, no, not like that. Anyway, I spoke to the girls, the Romanian girls. They have a room on the top floor of the hotel. At least I still live in town in a shared house. Their English is quite good but not good enough to do the waitressing work. They are all so upset though and have helped to get information. They need to know which rooms need cleaning and new bedding and which ones just need tidying so they check the hotel's booking system. They got the names of all the 'stag-men'."

Beth smiles, despite herself, at Sophia's terminology.

"We went on Facebook and checked out their names and matched them with faces. They are all at a lovely wedding the next day. Look!"

"Do you mind if we look at these on my computer screen? I struggle to see the details on your phone. What's the Facebook page called?"

Beth sits at the desk and pulls up a chair for Sophia. The next few minutes they glower at groups of smiling people with a pretty young woman in a typical meringue taking centre stage. The page belongs to Martin Sedgecombe. Beth looks for pictures of the previous day. Eight men with grinning faces stare at them. They are dressed in identical T-shirts with rude words on them. One of them also has a tiara on his head.

Beth recognises him as the groom. She doesn't recognise him personally but she knows Martin, Martin Sedgecombe; he is in Gavin's dart club. She struggles with a lump in her throat. No red balloon moment this time, no anger, just massive sadness. Martin, the always affable Martin was part of this gang!

"Look," Sophia points to a man in one of the larger crowd wedding photographs. "That's Peter Mezzo. These men are his friends. He's at the wedding. No wonder he doesn't want me to complain."

"Ok, that's why you don't think I should talk to him!"

"Yes, but," Sophia hesitates, then comes straight out with it, "I think they hate you Beth, after what you wrote. I heard him on the phone."

"Ok," Beth takes a deep breath. "One thing at a time. Now Sophia, can you identify which ones held you down and which ones made the, the, the comment, the...." Beth can't believe she is unable to say out loud what Sophia has only five minutes earlier told her in graphic detail, what these bastards did to her and her Romanian workmates. Her brain is mingling their rude comments with her article and pure hatred is entangling all her thoughts. Sophia comes to the rescue.

"Which one said we wanted 'some hot British cock'?"

"Yes, that."

"It was him, and those two held me down and those two held Marina down and those two held Irena down."

Beth doesn't recognise any of them except Martin. She checks the Facebook pages of all of them with total grim determination. The groom is a local lad, so are three of the others plus Martin. The other three are from the Manchester area. The British cock comment bloke is from Stockport. She looks at Sophia who is waiting expectantly as if Beth has all the answers. Beth looks inside her own head at an enormous void which keeps filling with tormentors who whirl around, escape and are replaced with other tormentors. She feels desperately alone.

Chapter 6 – Impotent

There is a beautiful smell emanating from the kitchen. Gavin is trying to make up to Beth. The table is already laid and the wine glasses filled.

"What's the occasion?" Beth is suspicious.

"I'm allowed to treat my beautiful wife, aren't I?"

"Thanks Gavin. I'm pretty done in. I've heard the most appalling tale today." She drinks half a glass in one go.

"Oh yeh? Who from?"

"Sophia."

"Sophia? Who's Sophia?"

"My student Sophia, I mentioned her the other day. She's Romanian, she's brilliant. But she's had an awful time of it and, you won't believe this, it actually involves your mate Martin Sedgecombe!"

"Martin! Ow, shit!" Gavin burns himself on the roasting tin. "Hang on, let me concentrate for a second."

"Do you need a hand?"

Gavin is running his wrist under the cold tap. "No, I'll be fine. Just a sec."

Beth uses the interlude to pour herself a top-up and gulps another half a glass in one go. She tops it again and feels her head relaxing. It's that lovely hovering feeling between being sober and being drunk.

"Ok, what's Martin done?"

"Well, he went to a stag do last weekend. One of his mates got married. They stayed at the new Glan-y-Môr, run by some guy called Peter Mezzo; do you know him by the way?"

"Heard the name, but don't know him!"

"Well, he's a right piece of shit. Sophia, my student, has been working as a receptionist, waitress, occasional chambermaid over the summer. There are a few more Romanian girls. There were three of them putting the final touches to one of the rooms when this bunch of louts came in and grabbed them, held them down, got their dicks out and one of them said, 'Oh you Polish girls, that's what you come to the UK for isn't it, to get some hot British cock!'"

"Did Martin say that?" Gavin nearly drops the plates on the way to the table.

"No, it wasn't Martin but he had his dick out just the same." Beth empties her glass. She wants to blot out her emotions properly.

Gavin moves the bottle to his side of the table. "Haven't you got a Garden Club meeting tonight?"

"Have I?" Beth is beginning to sound slurred. "See if I care!"

"Hey, this is not like you? You always care. You never miss a meeting."

"Well, you can go instead of me if you like." Beth stretches for the bottle.

"I'll phone Rhian to say you're not well. You're in no fit state to go in any case." Gavin takes the bottle and puts it on the other side of the kitchen. He recollects that the last time he saw Beth get deliberately drunk was when she found out she couldn't have children. That was about 15 years ago. She'd gone on a drinking spree for about three months until she'd come to terms with it in some way. He doesn't want a repeat.

Beth has her head on the table and appears to be asleep. Gavin takes Beth's phone so he can find Rhian's number. She has at least 40 unanswered voicemails and dozens of unread messages. He looks at Beth, her face blotchy, her mouth slightly sagging on one side, then at her phone. This is not his efficient Beth, his caring, capable Beth.

He quickly runs through the contact list and notes Rhian's number. He decides to send her a text from his own phone as he doesn't want a protracted discussion with her. He is well aware of how the Garden Club relies on Beth to organise all the outings and the speakers, events and, suddenly he is angry with everyone Beth knows, himself included. She's always been the reliable adult, the person who sorts things and now she's pissed off because she feels unwanted. He looks at her and notices her total vulnerability.

Gavin busies to get the meal on the table. He wakes Beth up with a strong coffee. "C'mon cariad, I'm dishing up. Please wake up. You've got the evening off. As soon as I've shut Anna's pigs up, and I'll deal with the chickens and the geese, then we'll curl up on the sofa."

Beth groans, she staggers to the bathroom, pees and washes her face. She eats her dinner in total silence. She's like a robot, the wine stilling the voices in her head.

"Do you want to watch telly or shall I put some music on?" asks Gavin once he's installed her on the sofa.

"Nothing, I just want silence."

"Well, do you want to tell me the rest of the happenings from that stag do lot?"

"About Martin and that lot? Oh God, shouldn't I be at the Garden Club?" Beth's brain is unclogging.

"I texted Rhian."

"So I should be?"

"You're having a night off."

"What about you? You're supposed to be playing darts!"

"I don't think I wish to face Martin, not yet, not tonight. I'm staying with you."

"Thank you darling."

Chapter 7 – Attacked

"How are you feeling this morning?" Gavin is dressed and looks fresh. He puts a cup of tea by the side of the bed.

Beth hauls herself on her elbows. Her head is thumping slightly. She sips her tea. Gavin is watching her intently from the bottom of the bed.

"Beth, I'm worried about you. You're taking this Brexit too much to heart. None of us knows what's going to happen. I," he hesitates about her drinking, "I don't want you to hit the bottle again." His face looks anxious as he forces himself to say it.

"What would you rather I do? Hit James Coburn? Hit Martin Sedgecombe? I'd rather not waste my fists on them. Wish I could get my hands on Nigel Farage."

The last sentence she says under her breath.

Gavin only hears the last two words. He has heard comments regarding Nigel Farage so many times in the last few months, he lets it pass.

"Thanks for the tea darling. Don't worry about me hitting the bottle; I have a battle to fight. Last night, well, it was all too much. I'd better get up. I have a Council meeting to attend at ten and I wish to pop in to see Anna."

Gavin looks relieved. "Will you be out all day?"

"Well, I never got the shopping done yesterday, nor did I do any tidying in my office, so I have to catch up today I suppose, oh, and contact Rhian, apologise, and," Beth feels her brain reeling. Catch up, catching up will take her more than a week even if she works every night.

"And?"

"And what?"

"You said 'and' after mentioning Rhian. So, what else do you need to do? I think that's enough for one day. Tell you what, I'll have dinner ready by six. Maybe we can relax on the sofa tonight, with you awake."

"So sorry!" Beth doesn't sound apologetic. She is cross, not with Gavin, but with the world. She is also cross with herself. She wants to stay in control, over her job, over her Council work, over events, over herself, especially over herself and she let herself slip yesterday. She recognises a weakness she doesn't like. She's never liked it in other people either. It's as if her body is like jelly; she can't grab hold of it.

Gavin is looking at her. She feels his eyes looking straight at her innards as if he can see all her secret thinking. "You haven't answered your text messages nor your voicemails. Why?"

"Are you checking up on me?"

"I just noticed them last night as I was looking for Rhian's number and," he emphasises the 'and', "I have noticed that you haven't been fiddling with your phone every few minutes. I'm not altogether obtuse you know."

Beth is struggling to get out of bed. She looks at Gavin who continues to fix his eyes on her. "Ok, I've let things slip. I needed a few days away from all that hassle after I had a really awful message."

"What really awful message? Why didn't you tell me about it?"

"It was a few days ago. I think it was a constituent unhappy about what I wrote in the newspaper."

"Have you still got it?"

"Probably. I'll check after breakfast and read the others. Promise, I'll get on top."

"So, was it just one?"

Beth's silence gives Gavin the answer. "Ok, I have to go now but I want you to promise to go through this awful stuff with me tonight. And, look, forget about Anna. She can cope without you for a day. See you later." Gavin bends down and gives her an affectionate kiss on top of her head.

Beth picks up her phone after breakfast. She touches the screen to read her messages as if the screen is going to bite her. She opens the messages that she is sure are ok. After 30 or 40 of these she tentatively opens one from a total stranger. Is it from a new supporter or another vicious death threat? She reads 'go hang urself u stupit bbb'

"That's it, you bloody uneducated plonker, can't even spell but tell me to, aaahhh!" Beth throws the phone on the sofa whilst her fists are flailing about. At that moment the land line rings. Beth looks at it in horror. She waits till the answer machine clicks in. 'Hi, this is Beth and Gavin, sorry we're not able to take your call, please leave a message after the tone, peeeew,'

"Oh, hi Beth, it's Rhian here, I got Gavin's text and thought,"

"Hi Rhian, I'm here," Beth grasps the phone. She sounds breathless.

"Are you ok Beth? You sound ill."

"I'm fine. Sorry about last night. You know I hate to let you all down."

"Don't worry Beth. I don't remember you ever missing a meeting. Are you ill?"

"I'm fine, honestly. I'll be there next week. Is there anything I need to do in the meantime?"

"We were hoping to find out more about the autumn trip to the Gardens on Anglesey. Apart from that, Kate took the minutes, she'll email them to you. Beth, are you sure there's nothing wrong?"

"Honestly Rhian, I'll be there next week with an update on the autumn trip as well as the winter one. Sorry, but I have to go. I need to be at a Council meeting in half an hour. See you."

Beth can't believe she's been so short with Rhian. She picks up her mobile phone as if it's a dog turd and gets her Council brief case. "Let's get this over and done with!"

Chapter 8 - Confident

"Councillor Evans, you have put together a report on the planning application for 26 affordable houses behind the Belle Vue. Have you anything to add?"

"No thanks, Mr Chairman, but if anybody has any questions, I'll be happy to offer detailed explanations."

Beth is on top of her own behaviour, her brain is clear, her mind is whirring away. No other Councillors have questions; her report was clear. There is a quick vote. Beth looks pleased with the result.

A small crowd is sitting at the back of the chamber. Beth is used to the press being there. There was nothing controversial in particular up for discussion today, no school closures, no wind turbines, no large supermarkets. She packs her papers and wanders to the exit. The small crowd follow her. She recognises the Herald reporter amongst them and gives him a warm smile.

"Councillor Evans, may we just have a quick word with you?" A young woman with a mass of dyed hair approaches Beth.

Beth suppresses her fear. She reminds herself that not all people voted Brexit, in fact almost half voted Remain. There are no nasty misogynists or racists lurking in every corner. Also, she's in a public space and feels herself protected by her fellow Councillors. She forces her most confident smile to her face. "How can I help you?"

"We read your article in the paper last week and wondered if you could give a talk to our group, Refugees Need Our Help. We're hoping to bring in some refugees from Calais and thought you might like to help."

"When would it be?" Beth realises that in her relief she

sounds almost abrupt.

"Well, we meet on Thursdays. It was the press chap here who suggested asking you." The young woman points to Chris Lavant, the Herald reporter.

"Hang on, let me check my diary." Beth starts to put her briefcase down, changes her mind and cheerfully says, "Why don't you all come to the canteen and we can discuss this over a cup of coffee."

Grunts of approval and smiles greet her so she leads the way. Chris Lavant grins after her.

"So, what exactly would you like me to talk about? I have not been to Calais, I mean to the Jungle. Of course I've been to Calais; I travel through it regularly to visit my family back home." There, she's used the word 'home' without a conscious thought. It stings. Beth finds herself momentarily confused.

"Are you ok?" The young woman who has identified herself as Cindy looks Beth intently in the eye.

"I'm fine. I don't know why I still call Belgium home. This is where I live. Yet I have always called Belgium home. It suddenly seems so weird."

"I understand. My mum is originally from Denmark. She always called it home, even though she's been here for more than forty years. But now she's confused too."

"Anyway, let's get back to your meeting. So, I'm happy to talk but need to know how long for and on what subject." Beth is back in business mode. She gulps her coffee down.

"How about integration? Like, what does it mean for you personally, your own experiences, how long did it take you to feel British, or do you actually feel British? Sorry, I'm Matt. I'm a history student."

"Thanks Matt, that sounds fascinating. I don't think I have a Power Point presentation on that." Beth is cringing secretly. She has a desperate need to get out in the fresh air. "Ok, next Thursday, eight pm, in the school hall on Market Street. I'll come and talk about integration. I look forward to seeing you all there. Sorry, but I need to get on now. Uni starts in only two weeks and I have lots to do." Beth smiles at the group and makes for the door.

Outside the Council offices she feels a tap on her shoulder. Beth jumps. "Oh, it's you Chris, you made me jump."

"So I see, and I'm not surprised. Your article last week caused quite a few comments on our Facebook page."

"I haven't looked. Are they really awful?"

"We don't allow the worst ones to be published. There are some real weirdos out there."

"You're not kidding."

"Have you had any personal attacks?"

"Chris, are you conducting a personal interview or are you fishing for an article?"

"Just interested."

"Sorry, I can't tell you anything right now. I'm not actually sure what to do."

"That's not like you."

"No, it isn't but then I've never been in this situation before.

I'll be in touch if I have anything to tell you. Will you be at this Refugees Need Our Help meeting next week?"

"Yep, I'll be there."

"I'll see you there then." Beth jumps in her car, waves at Chris and is off.

She manages to sort her office and answer all her Uni emails. On the way home she stops at the supermarket. Normally, she would nod hello to quite a few people, stop and talk to constituents either thanking her or asking her questions. Today Beth feels as if everybody is avoiding her. She grabs what she needs and heads for the check-out, convinced she's forgotten some important items. She stops at the end of the last aisle to check her list when she overhears a woman say, "That's her!" and a man respond, "She won't get elected again, stupid cow!"

The voices are coming from around the corner, from the next aisle she's just been in. She pushes her trolley round the corner and looks the couple directly in the eyes. She smiles haughtily and says: "Excuse me, may I just reach over there?"

Beth stretches to the top shelf. It's full of polishing material. She never polishes. She takes a random canister, puts it in her trolley, smiles again and says: "Thank you very much."

The man and the woman are both looking awkward. The man recovers first. "You're Councillor Evans aren't you?"

"That's right. Is there anything I can help you with?" Beth is almost enjoying their embarrassment. "Well, if there is, please contact me. Here is my card." She hands her card to the man. It's an unconscious ritual. She realises that she doesn't recognise them and has a sudden urge to find out exactly why he called her a stupid cow. She decides to play it a bit deviously. "Sorry, but I don't seem to know you. Are you actually constituents of mine? I thought I knew them all! Maybe you're new here?"

"We live on the other side of town. Mr Jones is our Councillor. He knows you and tells of you." The woman has found her voice.

"Ah, Councillor Jones, well I'm sure he loves to criticise me. He voted the new housing development through this morning though. Seemed pleased with my report." Beth recognises she's going over into defensive mode and stops herself. "Well, nice to meet you."

She walks off briskly to the check-out, takes out the polish and dumps it in an empty basket.

Chapter 9 – Abused

Gavin has dinner ready at six as promised, a lamb hotpot with the leftovers, no wine. Beth feels the hot gravy melting her cold mood.

"How was the Council meeting?"

"Fine, the housing development has gone through. How has your day been?"

"Pretty good till the tractor started playing up."

"Can you fix it yourself?"

"Hopefully, it's having the time to do it though."

"Do you need to buy another one?"

"It would swallow up a whole year's salary!"

"You mean my salary."

"You know that's what I mean!"

"Buy it if you need one." Beth doesn't want to go over the whole financial business again. The farm hardly makes any money. Without Beth's salary from the university and her income from being a Councillor, they would be scraping a living like so many Welsh farmers. Gavin receives Single Farm Payments from the EU but he hates the form filling. Underneath the caring farmer who is happy to cook and bring cups of tea in bed and even run Beth the odd hot bath, there is a proud independent male lurking who hates the fact that his wife earns more, much more, than him.

Beth finishes her hotpot. "Thanks Gavin, that was simply delicious. I'll make us some coffee."

"Oh, I popped over to Anna today, to see to her pigs and she was in there herself, coping very well. She doesn't have to wear the sling so is a lot more mobile. She sends her love. I told her you'd be seeing her at the weekend, that you're busy."

"Thanks darling. That's brilliant news."

"Talking about news, have you seen the news today?"

"Please don't depress me, I don't think I can cope with anything depressing."

"Well, it's party conference season and you're bound to hear a lot of depressing stuff in the next four weeks."

"Guess what, I've been invited by a group calling themselves Refugees Need Our Help to talk."

"When?"

"Next Thursday evening. I've said I'll do it. It'll be pretty informal."

"Hope you don't make any more enemies." Gavin ignores Beth's hurt look. "Are you ready to look at these offending messages now?"

Beth brings in the coffee. She hands Gavin her mobile phone. Her eyes fill up with tears. "You do it please, I can't face them. By the way, what was the news today you were going to tell me about?"

"Oh, don't worry, it was just Theresa May and her opening speech, pretty predictable really."

"I'll watch the late night news. If I feel up to it. Go on, open my messages. Just delete all the crap."

Gavin scrolls down and starts with the first missed one. It is over a week old. "This one is from Sophia."

"Oh no, why didn't I look at that one!"

"You haven't looked at any!"

"I know, I've been really stupid. Here, let me read Sophia's text. Oh shit, I need to sort her something urgently. Are there any more from her?"

Gavin checks the phone. "Here, another one from her. It's from two days ago."

"Let's see. Ok, I'll answer her now. I'll meet up with her in my office tomorrow. God, I feel so responsible for this young woman."

"Listen, if she's suffering more at the hands of that hotel bloke, she ought to go to the police. It's not your responsibility to sort this stuff out. You're getting enough abuse yourself!"

"I know Gavin, but she wants to go back to Romania and I think she should finish her degree first. Hang on a second, let me finish texting."

"Done? Right, let me carry on."

Gavin's eyes grow larger here and there. He mutters more to himself than to Beth about the childishness of some of the texts and the dreadful spelling. "All I can say is, it must make them feel better calling you all these ghastly names. Since when has anybody else called you BBB by the way?"

"I don't know. I had one this morning telling me to hang myself and calling me a stupid BBB."

"You checked your phone this morning? I thought you hadn't looked at it for over a week!"

"I thought I should stop being so silly but the first one I looked at made me want the trash the damn thing."

"Have you looked at your Facebook page?"

"I haven't posted much on there since Jo Cox's death. And I put stringent checks on it too, well I think I have. All I really look at now is family stuff."

"Ok, I'll Google it on my laptop. See what comes up, but first I'll finish these texts. I think you need to show some of these to the police. No wonder you've not been yourself lately, for God's sake Beth. You're getting the most horrible death threats and hate mail. It's totally unacceptable. Come here!"

Gavin goes to put his arm around Beth and with that she crumples. Her sobbing is uncontrollable and to Gavin's ears she sounds unearthly, hysterical. He doesn't know how to calm her. Suddenly he feels really angry. "Bloody Brexit, bloody referendum, bloody, bloody stupid people getting all het up about something so, so bloody stupid!"

Beth uncurls herself. Tears are gushing down her cheeks, snot drips from her nose. "Are you calling me stupid?"

"I think the whole bloody country should calm down a bit. It's stupid to get so worked up and...."

"Yeh, I'm stupid for getting all worked up. I'm getting death threats and get called every bloody name under the sun, but I should just stay calm!"

"I didn't mean it like that!"

"What did you mean then?" Beth blows her nose and is still

heaving.

"That none of us knows what is going to happen, none of us knows what the outcome of Brexit is going to be, so why get so angry?"

"Oh that's it. Beth should just shut up, not write articles in the Herald, be a good little foreigner, keep her opinions to herself and sit back and wait to see what the magnanimous Theresa May and her three musketeers will offer her!"

"No need to be so sarcastic!"

"I'll be as sarcastic as I like!"

"I just don't want you hurt." Gavin is calming down and is using his pleading voice.

"I don't want to get hurt either but since when is it ok in this country to threaten to kill somebody who has merely expressed an opinion?" Beth blows her nose again and picks up her phone. "Have you looked at them all?"

"Not yet."

"Well, I'll look at the rest myself. I can do without you making me feel rotten."

"I'm not trying to make you feel rotten; I just want to protect you." Gavin sounds exasperated.

"Well, what I want from you is that you stand up for me. It's what I've been asking for for months, but you won't do it. I have to do it all myself and now I'm being harassed and abused for simply sticking up for people like me who have only ever put themselves out to do good in this country. And what do I get from you? Anger at me!" Beth's voice reaches a hoarse pitch. "I'm going to bed. And you can go and sleep in

Anna's pigsty for all I care. Don't bother to disturb me!" Beth slams the door on the way out of the living room and stomps up the stairs.

Gavin can hear her cursing all the way. He holds his head in his hands. "BBB, my Beautiful Belgian Beth, who has changed my words?" He picks up his laptop and finds Beth's Facebook page. He then checks Martin Sedgecombe's page and scrolls through it. He spots a copy of Beth's article and there are a load of comments underneath it, all full of scorn and hatred for Beth, the Bloody Belgian Bitch.

Chapter 10 – Sarcastic

"Come in Sophia!"

Sophia enters Beth's office. She looks as if she hasn't slept for a week.

"Here, sit down. Do you want a coffee or a tea?"

"No thank you Beth."

"Sophia slumps in the chair. She looks with her great beautiful eyes straight at Beth. They are wet. "The other girls have gone back to Romania. There was a coach from Cardiff with spare spaces. There was such a row in the hotel. The boss has told me to go. Well, he told me to piss off back to Romania. I've been sleeping on the sofa at Jackie's place. I'm off next Saturday, by coach, so I've come to thank you and say goodbye."

"I hope you're not!" Beth is prepared for Sophia's announcement. "How would you like to finish your degree in Scotland? I've spoken to a colleague of mine and I can get you placed there. The atmosphere is quite different in Scotland."

"I don't know." Sophia hesitates understandably. She is not expecting this. "I don't think I feel up to it, another change."

"You don't have to make up your mind right now. I can tell you that there are two other Romanian students on the same course, a year below you, and there are many other European students. I think you'll settle in quite easily."

"Thank you Beth, thank you for what you've done for me."

"Look, here are all the details. I printed them off for you. The modules are not quite the same but there is enough overlap so that you can take all your credits with you. Your dissertation, they have agreed, can be supervised by me from a distance."

"Beth, I am in shock. You are doing this all for me?"

"Sophia, you are my star student. I want you to finish your degree. I want you to go back to Romania proud of having achieved, not defeated and deflated. And with me supervising your dissertation, I have an excuse to disappear to Scotland for a few days here and there."

"I will have that coffee." Sophia smiles through her tears, suddenly full of questions.

Back home Beth is humming a Scottish tune. She is slapping a curry together when Gavin walks in.

"You're sounding cheerful."

"I am. I have managed to remove a Romanian from Wales to Scotland where there is less anti-European sentiment. Her fellow countrymen, I mean female country women, have already returned to Romania. Soon, this country will be free from Romanians!" Beth is shouting as if she's on a political rally.

"Can you just drop the bloody sarcasm Beth! And I warn you, I'm not in a good mood; I didn't sleep well in the spare bed. Come on, can we just drop the subject for one night?" Gavin tries to give Beth a hug. "Please, can I give my beautiful wife a kiss? Can you please be your normal self?"

"I'll tell you when I'll be back to my normal self, whatever that means, when this country stops obsessing about immigrants and I start to feel at home again. And I'll tell you when I'll sleep with you again, when you start to stick up for your foreigner wife!" Beth stirs the curry. She gets two plates out of the cupboard, dishes up noisily. "There! Have some foreign food."

Chapter 11 - Passionate

"I would like to welcome you all and in particular I would like to welcome Councillor Beth Evans who is our keynote speaker this evening. Croeso i bawb. Croeso Beth!"

Cindy sits down, beaming a smile at Beth who stands up and faces the audience with her famous fighting look, a look of fearless defiance that has made her so successful as a Councillor and an academic.

"Diolch Cindy, thank you to Refugees Need Our Help for inviting me tonight. I actually haven't prepared a speech at all. If you had asked me a few months ago, I would have had an illustrated talk with statistics to boggle the mind but tonight I am going to talk about how I feel, how things changed for me on June the 23rd." Beth's face changes. She looks serious. She stops talking for a moment. She appears to be swallowing away tears. When she recovers and starts again, the audience is totally silent. Beth is able to speak quietly.

"I met my husband at a festival. It was Reading Festival. It wasn't long after that I moved here to Wales, a young woman in love. I didn't come here to be useful, I didn't come here to be an economic asset. Neither did I come here to scrounge benefits or to abuse the free NHS; I was not a health tourist." Beth stops briefly, examines the audience. Nobody seems bored.

"I didn't flee persecution. My Government in Belgium had been kind to me and I had a good education. When I was little I never felt Flemish, I never felt Walloon, I felt Belgian. By the time I was a teenager I had lots of German friends, French friends, Dutch friends, Irish friends and English ones. I had a friend who had fled from East Germany; he could speak at least six languages, even Welsh. By then I felt European. When I moved to Wales, for love, I moved at a time when young people conquered the world, not with ideas of colonisation like our predecessors, but with ideas of love and peace. Many young people in the generation just before mine had visited India, travelled through Afghanistan. My auntie had an Afghan coat. Travelling, seeing the world, learning from other cultures, all that was as normal in the 1980s as the World Wide Web is now. I felt cosmopolitan.

"When I first came to Wales, I worked on Gavin's farm. Gavin is my husband." Beth looks to the back of the hall and gives Gavin a quick smile. She continues. "Well, it was his parents' farm. The whole family welcomed me. Soon after, I went to work at the university, became a lecturer and a Councillor and the rest is history." Beth is quiet again. She looks at the audience and her expression becomes weary, painful. Her voice sounds a bit gruff when she starts again.

"So, where did it all go so wrong? Why are so many people in this country so anti-immigrant? Or have I been living with my eyes shut for the last 30 years?" Beth's voice is passionate by now, almost pleading. She takes a deep breath.

"So, I wrote an article in the Herald last month in which I explored the reasons for this apparent change of heart, the reasons why over 50% of people with a British nationality voted for Brexit. I mooted levels of education, poverty, unemployment, access to social housing. I was doing my best to understand this beast. I used fairly benign terminology but my conclusion was straightforward. I see Brexit as a negative, I regard anti-immigrant feeling as a backward step, I consider those who use the terms: asylum seekers, immigrants, NHS tourists, European migrants, and refugees; indiscriminately and interchangeably, as dangerous.

"I have received death threats as a result, I am now known as BBB, the Bloody Belgian Bitch, and you have asked me to come and speak about how I feel?" Her voice drops to an almost inaudible level. "I feel disappointed. I feel hopeless and helpless. I feel that all the dreams of the sixties and seventies, the dreams that inspired me and my friends, dreams of equality for black people, equality for women, an end to World Bank debts, an end to terrible famines in Africa, an end to tyrants, a world built upon democracy, openness, free speech, an educated world population; all those dreams seem to be just that right now, dreams. I feel they will never become reality. You want to know how I feel? I feel like I want to crawl into a cave and cry." Beth drops her head and hears the audience shift in their seats. Well, it's out now, her private made public. She looks up and the audience appears surprised by the fire in her eye.

Beth slams the table and shouts, "But I'm not going to. I'm not going to let a bunch of racists rule the world or stand by and allow Nigel Farage and his mates to dictate who should come into the UK and who shouldn't. I'm here in this hall tonight to help this group bring Syrian refugees to this part of Wales so that they can be housed safely, be educated safely, be helped to get their lives back together."

The audience erupts in applause. Beth smiles faintly.

"Sorry, you actually asked me to speak about integration and what it's been like for me." Beth's voice has altered again; it's her lecturer one, engaging but calm.

"For a long time there has been a discussion in this country between those who favour integration and those who favour diversity. By and large those discussions were about people who are visibly different, black people, Asian people, women wearing a hijab, Sikh men wearing a Dastaar. The debate has got more nuanced over the years. So you can be Black British, British Asian, even British Muslim. Immigrants who are seen to be different are expected to either behave like the British, or allowed, let me stress the word, allowed to keep some of their traditions but to what extent, that's our prerogative. By our I mean British white people.

"Many immigrants over the decades, probably over the centuries, have moved into places, areas of cities, where others like themselves were settled and some of these areas have become ghettos. It's one of the subjects I lecture on. As a planning expert I'm often asked if we can plan our way out of this conundrum. Before answering such a question I always want another question answered first: do we want to plan our way out of this? And that is a question for the whole of society, including the immigrant communities themselves. It's that question of integration or diversification. Can we have both? Can we have a mixture of the two? Is there a happy median?" Beth notices a few faces who are not entirely following her. She's ready to bring it back to her personal experiences.

"All my years of debating this and getting my students to debate this and for them to study real case scenarios, I was talking about other people, people with a different skin colour to me. I haven't lived in a separate Belgian community. I have always felt fully integrated into Welsh society. I eat the same food, mostly foreign." The audience laugh briefly; it's a welcome relief.

"I speak the languages, yes both of them, I dress like the British, join in the same organisations." Beth stops. She looks around her and waits for total silence. When she speaks again she talks very quietly.

"Anne Frank looked Dutch, went to school dressed like other Dutch girls, spoke Dutch, rode a Dutch bicycle, had Dutch friends. Why did she end up dying in a concentration camp? What had that young girl ever done to the Dutch, to the Germans, to the Nazis?" She waits for a few seconds. "Nothing. She was fully integrated. At her home prayers would have been said in Hebrew and on the Sabbath they would have gone to the synagogue, not to a Protestant or a Catholic church on a Sunday. That simple, single difference made her a scapegoat. Jews became scapegoats. Certain politicians are very good at exploiting problems in society, be it housing, employment, education, you name it, and they will find scapegoats. European migrants are the scapegoats now." Beth gazes round her and into people's eyes. A few people start to cheer her and chant: "Not in my name!" She holds her hand up to silence them with a smile.

"Thank you. I knew I would be talking to an immigrant friendly audience tonight. I am a lecturer and have a great deal of knowledge and understanding of this great issue called immigration." Beth swallows back a lump in her throat. "Yet, I am confused! I have never been so confused before in all my life. I have never felt so abused before in all my life. I have so many questions and so few answers. I also feel sad and angry." Her voice quivers. "And I feel scared. There has always been an element of anti-foreigner sentiment before Brexit but I never felt it levelled at me. Perhaps the element was much larger than I had ever noticed. Now it seems like the plutonium of all elements. It's explosive, it's lethal, it's dangerous!" She shouts the last few words. The audience stands up and applauds her. Beth waits patiently for them to stop. She closes her speech in a firm, quiet manner.

"We can all be positive about our ability to do our little bit for refugees, but," she emphasises the 'but', "I'm not trying deliberately to end on a negative note, but we must not kid ourselves. I felt at home for 29 years. That ended abruptly this year. And I'm Belgian, and as I've explained, not culturally that different from the British. It's going to be hard at times for the Syrian refugees. It is up to us, free thinking, tolerant people to protect them and to stick up for them, even at times at a personal cost. Thank you."

Chapter 12 – Surprised

"I have only managed to get 14 people to come along on the autumn trip. It's so weird; I wonder if we should cancel it."

"Do you think we should change the date?"

"We always go the last weekend of October! I'll ask the rest of the committee tonight. Can I have a look at your bulb catalogue?"

"Of course. I'll go and put the kettle on. The rest will be here soon." Rhian leaves Beth to peruse the gorgeous coloured pages of a Norfolk bulb catalogue.

"Evening Beth."

"Hi Brian, hi Liz, you're both ok?"

"Fine thanks."

The door opens and two other couples enter. Rhian brings the tea and coffee through. Liz puts some biscuits on a plate.

It's a cosy start to a normal Friday evening. Beth is relaxed. She has welcomed the new students today and she had an email from Sophia to say she's settled in well and has made a few friends. Beth puts the catalogue down and sips her coffee. "Are we expecting Harry and Josie?"

"They're running a little late. Harry says to start. He's bringing a new chap with him, a Peter somebody."

"Thanks Brian. Ok, has everybody had a look at the agenda? Can we sign the minutes as correct too?" Beth settles down for a routine evening. Gavin has gone to darts. She hopes for a quick meeting so she can go for a drink with Rhian afterwards and catch up with the latest gossip. "Ok then, thanks all, there are two main items on the agenda, the trip at the end of the month to Plas Cadnant and the request by the Council for the Gardening Club to take over the planting of the flower tubs next year."

The door opens and in walk Harry and Josie followed by a tall, handsome man in his forties. Beth recognises him immediately. Her face tenses. Rhian offers a chair and introduces herself.

"Hi, I'm Peter Mezzo, the new owner of the Glan-y-Môr."

"Would you like tea or coffee Peter?" Rhian is clearly enthralled by this newcomer.

"Hi, welcome to the Gardening Club. I am Beth Evans, the Chair. Can I introduce you to all the other members?"

Peter leans forward and shakes Beth's hand. It's a firm handshake. "I know who you are. You are Councillor Evans, the Belgian lady."

Bet you he thinks the BBB to himself Beth muses but she smiles at Peter and says: "That's right. Please help yourself to biscuits. Ok everyone, can we discuss item one on the agenda, the trip at the end of this month to Plas Cadnant on Anglesey. Only 14 people have signed up so far. We are used to at least 50. Yes Josie?"

"I think the trip might be a bit expensive for many folks."

"It's the same as last year, £25 including travel, entrance to the garden and a high tea." Rhian defends the costs.

"Thanks Rhian. Yes Simon?"

"I agree with Josie. I just think that a lot of people are very hard up this year."

"Thanks Simon. Do you think we should cancel it, put it off till the spring or should we go with the small band of keen gardeners who have signed up?"

"Oh, I don't know."

"Yes Peter?"

"I can advertise it in my hotel. Let's face it, £25 just about pays for a meal so it's really not that much to ask. How do you normally advertise these events? Sorry, I am not trying to tread on any toes here."

"Harry, would you like to explain to Peter, you're our membership secretary."

"Yes, well, we have nearly one hundred members. The committee organises a trip, well, Beth organises a trip, we just decide where to go and she actually, well, she does all the work you know and then it goes into the newsletter and members sign up to go. We do normally fill a coach."

"Yes Josie?"

"It will be a shame not to go, let's put it off till the spring. Maybe we can get a few new people to come or our members can save up."

"Shall we put that suggestion to the vote? Ok, all in favour of putting our trip off to the spring? Yes, that's carried. Right, next item is the Council's request for us to take over the planting of the large flower tubs. I can't take part in this debate so can I ask Rhian to chair please?"

Beth uses the break from chairing to reflect on Peter. He is certainly a charmer. He smiles winningly at everybody but especially the women. Rhian is clearly affected by him. Now that she's chairing, she is looking at him every other second to catch his eye, presumably in the hope of an approving glance. Beth thinks, what is she like?

The debate goes on for at least half an hour as nobody wants to take the responsibility but neither do they want to turn down this great opportunity. Beth knows what she would have said but, for a change, she enjoys the rest of the committee's feeble attempts at decision making. It's Peter who comes to the rescue. "Can we invite somebody from the Council, not a Councillor, but somebody from the correct department, to come and talk to us and set out exactly what would be required, what help we can expect from them, what budget we can aim for, etc."

There's a future chair, thinks Beth, a man with a business brain, a decision maker. Roll on the AGM!

"What a great decision you've all come to." Beth struggles to hide her sarcasm. "I'll invite the person Peter has suggested, I know the exact one. Well, if that is all, is there any other business? No, great, then I call this meeting closed."

Beth turns to Rhian to ask her to come to the pub. Something stops her. Rhian is busy collecting the cups, ably aided by Peter. Beth helps to put the chairs and tables away and picks up the bulb catalogue. She walks into the kitchen. Peter is washing up and Rhian is wiping. They are chatting away as if they've known each other for years.

Right, thinks Beth strangely nervous, "Rhian, are you ready to go for a glass of wine?"

"Of course, but guess what? Peter has invited us to have it in the Glan-y-Môr, he's going to treat us!"

Beth is stunned into an awkward silence. She puts down the catalogue and without a word just turns round and walks out of the hall. She can hear Rhian shouting her name but she jumps into her car and speeds off. No, she will not be entertained by Peter Mezzo in the Glan-y-Môr.

Chapter 13 – Insecure

"You're home early!" Gavin looks up from his computer screen. "What's up now?"

"That Peter Mezzo has joined the Gardening Club and Rhian is all gooey-eyed. I didn't want to go to his gaff for a drink."

"Shall I pour you a glass of wine?"

"Yes please, a large one." Beth is about to go to the study to drop off her stuff when she notices that Gavin is closing down his computer. "Don't stop on my account. I can watch the telly."

"It's ok, I was only looking at new tractors, well, I was dreaming really."

"Why don't we look at our finances and see if we can't get something a bit more reliable than you have now. It surely doesn't have to be a brand new one."

"Here you are Cariad. One glass of your favourite red." Gavin plants a kiss on her head.

"It's a few weeks since you called me Cariad."

"Well, it's been lovely sleeping with my darling Beth again. That week on my own was hell. I realise I've been a bit of a plonker. Here, move up."

"Thanks darling. It was so good to see you at the Refugees Need Our Help meeting. I saw you clapping. Was I as good as Kurt Cobain?"

"I needed to hear you, hear what you had to say to realise what a wonderful passionate wife I have."

"Thanks!"

"Oh, Chris Lavant phoned. You had literally just left. I told him you'd phone him back after the weekend."

"I wonder what he wanted."

"If it's urgent, he'll phone back. Relax and enjoy the weekend."

"Oh, I have lots of preparation work for Uni to do but I am determined to visit Anna. I thought Sunday morning. You know we were going to visit that garden on Anglesey at the end of the month? Well, trip's off or at least postponed till the spring. So, perhaps we can go, you know, just the two of us."

"Yeh, maybe, why is it off?"

"Not enough people interested. Of course new boy Peter Mezzo suggested we can advertise the trip in his hotel." Beth tries to copy Peter's voice in an exaggerated manner. She drops her voice so sudden she surprises Gavin. "I tell you, I'm not standing for Chair at the AGM."

"You're kidding me!"

"No, I think Mr Mezzo would be an excellent Chair and I'm sure he can organise trips too."

"Hey, hey, you're not standing down because he's been to one meeting. He'll probably never turn up again."

"You could be right. I don't think he's even a member. Still, he's that kind of cocky bloke who's got plenty to say for himself."

"You mean cocky bloke who's full of bollocks but never does

anything."

"Don't know really; he was very personable but I instinctively distrust the bloke. He clearly gets things done. He's got that hotel up and running and, let's be honest about it, it was a dump before."

"Listen to you defending him! So why didn't you go there for a drink with Rhian?"

"Cos I don't want to cavort with the enemy!" Beth pronounces the word enemy as if it is an enemy itself.

"The enemy?" Gavin sounds totally puzzled.

"Yes, the enemy, he's a Brexiteer through and through. He treated those Romanian girls abysmally. Who knows, he may even be responsible for some of the awful emails and tweets I've been getting."

"Maybe he's trying to put the whole Brexit thing behind him, move on you know, maybe he feels sorry for....."

"Sorry for me, for Sophia, for her friends!" Beth's voice is raised.

"No, no, please, let's not start the old argument again. I mean, maybe he is sorry for how the whole thing got out of hand and he is trying to build bridges."

"Maybe, or maybe he is trying to figure me out, demean me in public."

"Now you're being paranoid."

"That's a ridiculous thing to say." Beth jumps up. She carries on shouting. "I can't just put it all behind me as if nothing has happened at all! I'm still not one iota clearer as to my status. I can't carry on pretending nothing changed on June the 23rd. Just go, oh well," Beth carries on talking in an animated Disney film voice: "I lost, and all the people who voted Remain, well, they lost with me and now we're all going to shake hands with the Brexiteers and say: 'Well done, you've won and we've lost but we're going to get along just fine because we're the happy losers' and those of us who will get sent home will say: 'Thank you so much for letting us live in your country but now it's time we went back to where we belong.'"

Gavin is laughing and Beth joins in despite of herself. "Oh, sod Peter Mezzo and sod the Gardening Club!"

"That's a good pun Beth."

"What is?"

"Sod!"

"Sod? Oh, yes, very funny!"

"You made the pun."

"I didn't realise. Maybe I can get a job as a stand-up comedian on board the P&O ferry."

"You're not going anywhere, you're staying with me."

Beth sits back down. "Thanks for your confidence darling. But, in all seriousness, I am going to stand down at the AGM. I've been chair for, what, 13 years now, was the secretary before that, I've done my bit. If the club falls apart, so be it. The trouble is, it's such an awkward time, what with the Council asking the club to take over the big flower tubs. And I can't even speak about it."

"You can talk to me."

66

"Yes, I know but you can see the situation I'm in. I don't want the club to take on something they can't really cope with. It'll be me out there planting the tubs, me and Rhian, oh and maybe Harry will put in a few bulbs. And there will be the endless arguments about what should and shouldn't go in, and the people with the biggest gob will be the least available, and then there's the watering, who is going to volunteer to do that?"

"And now tell me the problem from the Council's point of view."

"No money, simple, no money. We need to get rid of services, cut our budgets. The argument's simple. If keen gardeners want to see pretty tubs full of flowers, if tourists are attracted to our town because of pretty tubs full of flowers, then let those who feel strongly about it, do it. The Council has more important jobs to do like sorting out social care for the elderly, extra help in schools for kids who need it, buses, libraries, swimming pools, you name it, these things are all higher up the agenda."

"Fair enough!"

"There must be an answer to this conundrum. Maybe I don't have the answers for anything anymore. I'm thinking of not standing for the Council next May either."

"Beth! You don't mean it!"

"I do mean it Gavin. I'm serious. And, let's be honest, I'm still not sure whether I'll be allowed to stand."

"Why on earth not! You've been a Councillor for over nine years." It's Gavin who's shouting now.

"You really haven't got your head round this one yet, have you Gavin? I'm a bloody foreigner now! I was never treated like one before Brexit but now I am. Theresa May has not told us what rights the likes of me will have so I have to be realistic. Also," Beth's voice goes quiet.

"Also what?"

"Will I win my seat again? Am I really up for coping with not winning? So many people hate me now."

"You won easily last time!"

"Yes, but that was four and a half years ago. It seems a lifetime away. I feel so unsure about so many things now." Beth sips her wine and stares into space. "Let's change the subject. When are you going back to darts?"

"Oh, probably next week. If you can face Peter Mezzo, I can face Martin Sedgecombe."

Chapter 14 – Exposed

"Good morning Beth. How's the new intake?"

"Morning Christine. They're great, thank you. A few quiet ones but a few very vocal ones too. I'm looking forward to working with them."

"Any news of Sophia?"

"She's settled in well, thanks. I was thinking of having a few days in Scotland in reading week."

"I don't see why not. I wanted to talk an idea through with you. Do you mind?" Prof Christine Maynard-Jones points to the empty chair. Beth nods and smiles.

"No, of course, take a seat."

"I read your article in the Herald, when was it, September?"

"August actually."

"Ok, and I also read the report on the Refugees meeting, where you were the keynote speaker and I thought….."

Beth is beginning to worry. Her Head of Department usually asks Beth to come to her or waits for a formal meeting. She holds on to her smile in a determined way to fight off tears.

"I thought that our Department should run a series of Public Lectures on the theme of Brexit, UK Laws and what it all means in practice."

Beth's fear levels reduce and with it the tension in her face. She realises she hasn't fooled Christine. "That sounds like a brilliant idea."

"Good. I need to run it past the Vice Chancellor but this is what I had in mind." She hands Beth a piece of A4 paper with four clear paragraphs. Beth reads the first one.

"You would like me to hold the first lecture?"

"I can't think of a better person. As you can see I've put myself down to do the second one on Environmental Law in relation to SAC's and SSSI's, Rhodri to lecture on Energy Policy and the Paris Agreement, and Cerys to do the final one on Planning Policy Guidance, Health and Safety Policies and the implications of changing these. Don't take this the wrong way but I think we need you to hold the first lecture as you'll pull in the crowds. You are the only one in our Department with such a public profile. We could bring in speakers from outside but I firmly believe we have plenty of expertise ourselves."

"Sure, you're right. What are you ultimately hoping to achieve? What is your real objective with these lectures?"

"To educate the masses. People have voted Brexit, or Remain come to that, without really understanding the implications."

"Wish we'd held these a year ago."

"That's as may be. We are where we are and now everybody has to understand that it's a complex process to unpick laws and put them back together again. All and sundry are after different outcomes. We have so much detailed knowledge in our Department. Let's impart it." With that Christine rises and leaves Beth's office.

Beth reads the proposal carefully. Christine has scheduled the lectures for the early part of the second semester so Beth has a few months to prepare. She can probably put it together in an evening; she is the expert in Planning Law after all and knows all about Human Geography, Movement of People and what it means for housing developments. She is determined to use her lecture to showcase how amazing the EU has been in improving life for the ordinary UK citizen. As she is calmly pondering, she checks her list of things to do. First, phone Chris Lavant. Beth's feeling positive and wary at the same time. She's still examining why she feels this way when Chris answers the phone.

"Chris Lavant, Herald, how can I help you?"

"Bore da Chris, good morning, it's Beth Evans. You phoned me Friday and spoke to my husband."

"Hi Beth, hope you had a good Gardening Club meeting."

"I did, thank you," she lies. "What can I do for you?"

"I was wondering if I could come and interview you for our Profile Column. We haven't profiled you before and I was thinking how remiss of me." Chris sounds charming as usual. Beth knows his style.

"What exactly would you need to know about me that you don't already know?"

"Oh, a few skeletons in the cupboard." Chris can hear Beth groan quietly. "Just kidding. No, you know this column is to write things about people in powerful positions in our community that interest ordinary people, like, what makes you tick, why are you so passionate? We want to get to know the real Beth behind the professional, organised, efficient person we know. Tell us about your childhood experiences, tell us how you felt when you got those abusive emails."

"Feel!"

"Feel?"

"I'm still getting them!"

"Sorry, I didn't know, I thought they must have stopped."
"Never mind, when do you want to do this interview?"

"You tell me when you're available. You're the busy person."

"How about Wednesday afternoon?"

"Great. Where shall I meet you?"

"My home ok with you?"

"Great! Shall we say 2pm?"

"I'll have the kettle on. See you then. Bye." Beth puts the phone down. Butterflies are flapping wildly in her stomach. She, the unflappable Beth, is nervous, not just about this interview, but about what people will make of her, about the next lot of threats, about what Gavin will say. She feels wretched. Why didn't she just tell him to get lost! She knows why. She has to use this opportunity to justify her views. She actually feels she has to justify herself, her behaviour, her existence here. She will have to take the flack.

On her way home she decides to pop into Anna's place. She never did visit her on Sunday. It's not that she's any busier and has less time for Anna; it's more that she doesn't know what to talk about. All she wants to discuss is herself, her post-Brexit situation, her feelings of despair, and she can't talk about any of those with Anna. Nor with Gavin really, she muses, because he's had enough of it. Nor with Rhian, because she's supping with the devil. I'll just have to talk about the weather, won't I, or pigs!

"Anna, hi Anna, are you in for a visitor?"

"Beth, come in dear, oh how lovely to see you."

"Sorry that I haven't been for a while."

"You're busy I know."

"How are the pigs?"

72

Chapter 15 – Confused

The phone rings as Beth walks into the house. It's dark. Gavin is nowhere to be seen or heard. Beth lets the phone go to the answer machine. She hears Gavin's sister's voice. She's asking about their Christmas plans.

"It's bloody October!" Beth shrieks out loudly. She walks into the kitchen, puts the kettle on and looks into the fridge. Gavin must still be busy outside. She quickly throws a curry together whilst drinking her tea. She has a gut feeling it's going to be a difficult evening.

The outside door opens. Gavin is whistling.

"Hello darling. There's tea in the pot."

"Lovely, my feet are frozen. We have a problem with the drains."

"Here, warm up." Beth kisses Gavin. "Oh, bloody hell, you pong like…."

"Like a blocked drain, there's nothing like it."

"Go and have a shower! Dump your dirty clothes outside the bathroom; I'll shove them straightaway in the machine."

"Ok, ok, can I just drink my tea? I'm bloody knackered!"

"Sorry! Anyway, I'm cooking a curry. It should be ready by the time you smell civilised again."

Twenty minutes later they are enjoying their meal when Gavin's mobile rings. "It's Gwenith. I'll phone her after dinner."

"She left a message on the answering machine. She wants to

know our Christmas plans."

"You've spoken to her?"

"No, I just listened to the message and thought you could deal with it. Honestly, Christmas! It's over two months away! What the hell does she think we have Christmas organised this early for. I've only just started back at Uni!"

"You know what Gwenith's like."

"Yes, unfortunately I do."

"Come on, let's not go through all that again."

"No, let's not. Tell me what needs to be done about the drains. And which ones are broken?"

"The ones from the cowshed to the pit. I've fixed them, well temporarily, I had some spare pipes."

"Well, that's brilliant. Have you had a look on-line yet for another tractor?"

"Not yet. I thought I might do it this evening. How was Uni?"

"Lovely thanks. Professor Maynard-Jones has come up with a lovely idea to do some public lectures on Brexit. She's asked me to give the first one. I've also spoken to Chris Lavant. He's coming here on Wednesday to write a profile on me. Oh, and I popped in to see Anna on my way home."

"How is she?"

"Coping just fine."

"I don't get you Beth."

74

"What exactly don't you get?"

"Last Friday you were talking about giving up the Gardening Club and the Council and now you're going to be interviewed for a profile and you're going to give a public lecture. Do you want these abusive messages to stop or not?"

"Of course I want them to stop. But I was ready to give in to the bullies in August and now I think they can just take a hike."

"That's not what you said last week. I still had to go through your text messages for you. Friday you wanted to give it all up and now you're doing the opposite!"

"Hang on, Friday I said I wanted to give up the Gardening Club and wasn't sure if I wanted to stand again for the Council; the public lecture is for the Uni and the profile is for me." Suddenly Beth stops talking. She hasn't really given it proper attention. She instinctively said yes, thought it would benefit her in some weird way. Will she actually benefit from this exposure? Will she see the copy before it goes to print? Will she be able to get the message out that she wants to get across and what message is that exactly? She suddenly feels she agreed to this on a whim.

Gavin is looking at her expectantly. "Every time you make a scene in public, you end up with more threatening calls and emails. You don't want the police involved, you want the abuse to stop but you keep putting your head above the parapet."

"I thought you were keen for me to stand again for the Council."

"Well, yes but…."

"But you don't want me in public talking about Brexit any

more. If I can just stick to talking about housing developments and rubbish collection and libraries!" Beth has stopped eating and is banging her knife and fork on the table. "Do you know, I don't talk to Anna about Brexit."

"Why?"

"Because she looks shifty."

"What's that supposed to mean!"

"When I was really upset in June after the result, she had a guilty look on her face. I just know she voted Brexit but she doesn't want to upset me and that's why she looks shifty whenever I've brought up the subject. Like she hopes I'll talk about something else please, so we can carry on as if nothing has happened." Beth is almost breathless as she gushes out what's been bothering her these past few months with regards to Anna.

"Look, if Anna did vote Brexit, she probably voted for a reason that's nothing to do with you being a foreigner."

"That's what they all say, well, to my face anyway." Beth puts on her exaggerated voice again. "'Oh, I'm not a racist but I don't like all these immigrants.' 'You mean people like me.' (said in her Beth voice but rather bluntly) 'No, I don't mean people like you.' 'Well, I am an immigrant.' 'But I don't mean people like you.' 'You mean people with a black skin!' 'No, I don't mean that.' 'Well, what do you mean?' 'I mean people who come and take our people's jobs.' 'I have a job. Have I taken one of your people's jobs?' 'No, I don't mean your job, I mean the people who come here and get our benefits.' 'Oh, so it's not the jobs but the benefits.'"

Beth looks at Gavin's patient face. He's heard the Beth dialogue-monologue many times before this year and he allows her to indulge in it. It calms her usually.

"What I actually said was, not everyone who voted Brexit did so over the immigration issue. There were other reasons you know, and Anna may well have had other reasons. If she voted Brexit! You're just making an assumption."

"Yeh, right!" The fight has gone out of Beth. She leaves the table and slumps in front of the telly. "You'd better phone Gwenith!"

Beth turns the telly on. She can hear Gavin talk from the kitchen. The news from Syria is more dire than ever. Beth makes a mental note to discuss the refugee crisis in her profile. The US election is the next main item. As soon as Donald Trump's face shows, she reaches for the off button. She just can't stand his blatant anti-Mexican and anti-Muslim stance. "Intolerant git!"

"Who? Me?" Gavin walks in.

"No, that arsehole Donald Trump! God, please let the polls be right this time. I really can't bear the thought of him being President."

"No, horrid thought. Anyway, I've spoken to Gwenith. They've been invited over to New Zealand, to Owen's brother for Christmas."

"Well, that's a nice thing."

"Yes, they need to book a flight soon or they won't get a good deal. They want to go for six weeks, take the kids, have the holiday of a lifetime."

"Can't blame them. So, why did she need to speak to you so urgently?"

"They need to sort out how to have the farm looked after. It will be lambing time when they're away."

"So? They just need to pay someone to stay there."

"That makes it unaffordable. They've asked me if they can bring the sheep here and that I take care of the lambing."

"You've got to be joking! You couldn't look after Anna's two pigs for a few minutes a day in July and now you're willing to take on, what a hundred or so sheep?"

"One hundred and forty ewes are due to lamb in January."

"You have said no I hope."

"I've said yes."

"You gave up on sheep three years ago because you couldn't cope! And neither could I! How many times did you get me up to help with a breech birth?"

"I know Beth, but, listen please. If they pay someone to stay at Wern Fawr, well, one person won't be enough. They would need three to cover the rota. If the sheep are here, I can cover most of the time and pay one labourer to do a few shifts so I can get some sleep and go to market. The cows will be indoors so they're minimum work."

"You say you're going to pay for a labourer."

"No, of course not; Owen and Gwenith will pay."

"For the whole six weeks?"

"For the most hectic two weeks. Most of the ewes are due the second and third week in January." Gavin is looking uncomfortable.

"I knew it!" Beth is getting very annoyed. "Gwenith and Owen and their perfect children will go swanning off to New

Zealand for a perfect family holiday and Beth and Gavin can be sheep sitters!"

"Beth, you're not being fair. You know Owen hasn't seen his brother since the wedding, what, five years ago! You told them last Christmas that they should go and now they are going you're being so cross about it. I don't know what's got into you." Gavin plonks himself in an armchair and looks at Beth who is beginning to cry.

"I don't know either. I'm just so pissed off with so many people and feel so resentful. I've always gone out of my way to help others but I just feel so bloody unwanted that I've got my hackles up all the time and feel like telling everybody else to piss off like they tell me to piss off."

Gavin moves to the sofa and puts his arm around Beth. "I need you. You're not unwanted by me."

Beth struggles to get out of his embrace. She wipes her face and shouts, "You know very well what I mean. I can't turn the news on or there's somebody spouting off about bloody immigrants this or bloody immigrants that. And it's me they're talking about. After 30 years of slugging my guts out, I can be talked about like a piece of shit, a bloody bargaining chip. So, sorry, yes, I am a different person from last year. That's what's Brexit has done."

Gavin tries again to put his arms round her. "Beth, I hate to see you so upset. Nobody can demand you leave the country."

"Can't they! Perhaps not, but they can make my life impossible so my life here won't be worth living!"

"Let's wait and see, shall we?"

"No, I don't want to wait and see. I want to know now! I'm

fed up with living in limbo." Beth gets off the sofa and starts to walk to the kitchen.

Gavin calls after her. "Beth, it will be ok. And, please, Owen's sheep will also, I mean, we'll manage. I'll manage."

Beth turns round at the door. Her eyes are blazing but her voice is calm. "Do you know how Owen and Gwenith voted?"

"Why, what's that got to do with anything?"

"I know they're strong Plaid supporters but they didn't put a Remain poster up, did they? And when I offered them one, Gwenith scoffed. Do you know if they were Brexit supporters?"

"I, I, I'm not sure." Gavin's hesitation betrays his knowledge.

"They voted Brexit, didn't they? Well, as far as I'm concerned, they can get stuffed. I shall not be helping with their sheep, nor do any extra cleaning, cooking or shopping, or Christmas card writing, so you can spend all hours in the lambing shed. Forget it!" She slams the door and leaves Gavin sitting with his head in his hands.

Chapter 16 – Uncertain

"There's a letter for you." Gavin hands Beth a plain white envelope. "Can we please start again? Beth? Please? Can we be civilised over this whole Brexit thing? I'll phone Gwenith and say they have to pay for extra help. Sorry Beth, you're right. I've been taking you for granted. Please?"

Beth is looking at him but she doesn't answer. Gavin hates her silent anger.

"Here, open your letter. Do you want me to make you a cooked breakfast?"

Beth pours herself some coffee and puts some bread in the toaster. "No thanks, toast is enough."

She slides the letter open and reads rapidly, slams the letter on the table and exclaims, "Typical! Pass the buck!"

"Do you mind?" Gavin reaches over to the letter. Beth shrugs her shoulders and prepares her toast.

"Beth, this is appalling! You're a tax payer and a National Insurance payer. They can't do this!"

"Well, obviously they can. I've been saying this since before the vote. Mind you, can you imagine if we're going to end up with a different system in Wales to England? Oh, and Scotland will of course have a more favourable system too. All the European Union citizens will want to move to Scotland or Wales. That will sort out the shortage of doctors here." Beth's tone is full of bitterness and sarcasm.

"What are you going to do? Write to Vaughan Gethin?"

"Of course I'm going to write to him. Not that he will give a definitive answer. He'll be like all the others, pass the buck. I feel like I'm the parcel in pass the parcel. Look, I've got to go. I'm likely to be home quite late." Her voice is less belligerent but not friendly either.

"At least let me give you a kiss. And I promise, I'll phone Gwenith and say we need more temporary helpers."

"Why don't you offer to find three or four for the price of one or two?" Beth has returned to sarcasm. The grin on her face is not conciliatory.

"What? How?"

"Get them from Eastern Europe!" With that Beth walks out of the kitchen.

Two minutes later she walks back in and picks the letter off the table. Gavin is staring out of the window. He senses her looking at him. His voice is strained. "Beth, I know you're having a difficult time and things are very unpleasant for you but can you please stop taking it all out on me. You keep slamming doors, making cutting remarks, I just don't know what to say any more as I'm scared you're going to take offence."

"I know, I'm aware of it. Sorry! See you later." Beth goes over to Gavin and gives him a hug.

"We are ok, aren't we?" Gavin looks deep into Beth's eyes. "Please don't tell me you're fed up with me too."

"No, it's not you. It's this whole rotten situation. I just feel so lost, so unsure of myself, so I'm lashing out at you. I know it's not fair." Beth kisses Gavin. "I really must go. I want to write to Vaughan Gethin before the Council meeting. I have two lectures this afternoon and I'm meeting my new students in their first tutorial at five. I'll be home about seven."

82

"I'll have dinner ready."

"Thanks."

The Council meeting is an odd experience for Beth. She realises she is hardly contributing. A large supermarket chain wants to build an enormous shop in one of the most unsuitable places. She had received the pre-planning proposals a week previously like the other Councillors. She listens to them all putting in their pennyworth's. A year ago she would have been the Councillor with the most to say. Her expert knowledge on planning has always been valued. She senses other Councillors looking at her, desiring her to speak but she feels empty about the proposals. As far as she is concerned they might as well be talking about a new supermarket in China or Brazil. The place she has loved for three decades feels alien in her heart.

The Chair of the Council forces her to air her thoughts. She lies. "I shall take the proposals home and offer an opinion at next week's meeting. I've heard what you all had to say."

One of her fellow Lib Dem Councillors gives her a look of total disbelief. He was clearly expecting her to crush this plan straightaway. She knows she can demolish it there and then but she is still in this perverse mood she keeps finding herself in. She wants everyone to wait; she wants them to suffer, she doesn't want to give of herself any more.

Her university work lightens her spirit. Two lectures fly by. Her new students are full of enthusiasm. She laughs and jokes with them as if she hasn't a care in the world.

On the way home she thinks about the words Gavin spoke to her that morning. "We are ok, aren't we?" She stops the car at the viewing point and gets out. This is the first time in 30 years that she has stopped here. The view is truly awesome, hills of different hues in one direction with the sun setting over the sea in the other direction. Lights are twinkling from every small settlement for miles and miles around.

She gets her phone out and takes 360° photographs. Tears are running down her cheeks by the time she is on her last photograph and faces the sunset again. A sudden urge to send this blur of orange to her mother grips her but her mother doesn't do Facebook or email or twitter; she's a woman in her nineties who has never coped with technology.

Beth takes a deep breath, wipes her tears and opens her own Facebook page. Standing on the top of this hill she is exposed to the elements from four directions. Her exposure on Facebook is worldwide it seems. Comments from total strangers who question her validity to live in Wales, question her validity to open her mouth or, even worse, question her validity to live, mingle amongst the comments from her supporters, known and unknown. Beth blanks them all. She opens her list of friends and finds one she's looking for, an old school friend who lives near Beth's mum outside of Brussels. Beth writes a quick message and attaches the photograph.

"You're late! I was getting worried about you."

"The sunset was so stunning, I just had to stop and capture it. Look!"

Chapter 17 – Deluded

"Tea? Coffee?"

"Just some water please. I never drink on the job."

Beth disappears to the kitchen to get some water. On the way there her eyes lift skywards. She's always known Chris Lavant to be a jokey kind of fellow. Trouble is that his jokes are never funny. Also, she's never sure whether he says things in order to have a slight dig because he knows something or because he's watching for a tell-tale reaction. Let's beware of this trickster, she thinks to herself.

"Ok Beth, now I'm sure you've read plenty of other people's profiles before, so you must realise the sort of things I'm after."

"Yes, you told me, skeletons in the cupboard."

Chris guffaws.

"Did you know I've been a heavy metal fan for a long time? Is that a skeleton?"

"Not quite. But did you take drugs?"

"Are you asking me about legal or illegal drugs?"

"I'm sure the readers won't be interested in the legal ones."

"No, funny that, isn't it?" Beth looks Chris in the eye steadily.

"Anyway, let's start at the beginning. You were brought up in Belgium. Tell us a bit about your childhood."

"Sure. I was born in a small town on the outskirts of Brussels. My mother still lives in the same house. I went to school there, both primary and secondary. I worked hard, never got into trouble. I went to university in Antwerp and that's where I really got into heavy metal music. I bought records and tapes and later CDs and went to concerts. There was a large group of us who would go to every concert we could possibly go to."

"Was your dress code that of a heavy metal fan?"

"You mean long hair, heavy metal T-shirts, lots of black eye make-up?"

"That sort of thing, yes."

"Of course. I actually still have a large collection of T-shirts in my chest of drawers in my bedroom. They are slowly disappearing as I wear them out in the garden."

"And what about headbanging?"

"I think I was one of the best headbangers around. I had very long hair, dyed jet black, which I could fling up and down with gusto."

"So what about the drugs then? The illegal ones? Surely drugs were a large part of that scene?"

"They were, but I wasn't interested in taking any. Some of my friends took lots of drugs from cannabis to downers and at times ended up in A&E but not me, I preferred a drink."

"You liked to drink?"

"That's a bad way of putting it. I enjoyed a few glasses of dark beer. In Belgium we have beautiful dark beer brewed by monks, Trappist monks. It is sold in large round goblet kind of glasses and it's very strong. When I moved to the UK, I started drinking Guinness which is not dissimilar but nowhere near as nice, well in my opinion. I prefer a glass of red wine these days. I don't do headbanging any more either."

"So what made you move to Wales?"

"When I finished my degree I celebrated by buying a ticket to Reading Festival. There was a group of about a dozen of us. We travelled over on the ferry to Dover and made our way to Reading. It was the first time I'd been. I'd been to other festivals on the continent before, Germany, the Netherlands, but never to the UK. At Reading Festival I met Gavin. We hit it off straightaway."

"How good was your English?"

"Pretty perfect. One of my lecturers at the university was English and he was happy to converse with us in English, help us translate songs, write our own, you name it. He was into heavy metal too. And also, don't forget, I had been learning English at school from the age of ten."

"What language did you speak at home and at school?"

"My mother is a Walloon so her first language is French, my father is Flemish so he preferred speaking Flemish. They both spoke both languages and in school we spoke both. In that part of Belgium it is the norm to speak both. It's quite similar to Wales where it's normal for people to speak Welsh and English, don't you think?"

"Quite so. You yourself have also learned to speak Welsh since moving here I understand."

"I have. Rwy'n siarad Cymraeg, diolch."

"Do you speak any other languages?"

"I speak Spanish, Italian and some German."

"That's incredible!"

"To me, it's normal. My school did exchanges with Spain and Italy. I loved going there so I went every summer for extra time."

"Tell me a bit about your early time in Wales."

"I moved here in the spring of 1986. I was 23. Gavin's parents were both alive then and they owned and ran the farm. Gavin worked on the farm, full time though. I wanted to learn the ways of the farm and to learn Welsh so I asked if I could simply join in and asked them to only speak Welsh with me. It really is the only way to learn I think. They thought I was lovely. We married in the autumn and I applied to the Uni here to do a PHD. I was accepted and here I am!"

"You make it sound so easy."

"When you're young and in love and when you're ambitious and full of hope, everything looks and feels easy. I also truly believe that we were idealists in those days and that everything seemed possible so we weren't easily daunted."

"I heard your speech at the Refugees Need Our Help meeting. I've heard you speak on many other occasions at Council meetings and once at the Lib Dem conference. You always come across as very passionate. Where does this passion come from?"

"Oh lord, what a question! I'm sure I've been influenced by some amazing people. My father was a keen trade unionist; he was always talking about unfair wages and unfair working conditions. Of course we always watched the news together so as children we learned at an early age about the inequalities in the world. I remember the war in Vietnam and later Pol Pot in Cambodia. When I was studying in Antwerp it was the height of the Ethiopian famine. To me Bob Geldof is a real hero and Midge Ure. They at least tried to do something positive about an awful situation. That taught me to never sit on my backside and do nothing if I can make just the slightest difference. But the person who has influenced me the most is my aunt."

"Go on, tell me about her."

"Auntie Cecelia, Auntie Celie we called her, although once I went to Uni I just called her Celie. She wasn't much older than me."

"Wasn't?"

"She died two years ago. She had lung cancer. She was only in her sixties but she had lived life to the full. She was a true hippy. She travelled everywhere, hitch-hiked to India, God, she was fearless. In the 1980's she went and helped out in South Africa in an orphanage for children with Aids. She lived every day as if it was her last and every one of them mattered. I have her old Afghan coat and some wonderful trinkets she brought back from her travels."

"How about a photograph?"

"I'll dig some out and email them to you."

"That'll be great. You don't happen to have some of you in your AC-DC T-shirt?"

"I'll find you something."

"Can I go back to your political career? When did you join the Lib Dems?"

"In the late 1990s. I heard one of their MPs speaking about the Palestinians and their plight, and I thought she was great. Then, one of our local Councillors happened to talk to me about a particularly tricky planning application and he persuaded me to come along to a local meeting."

"And you've been a Councillor since?"

"Since 2007. I stood in 2002 but was not successful. I've been a Councillor now for nearly ten years."

"Will you be standing again next year?" Chris notices a slight hesitation. It's so momentary and Beth is so confident in her answer that he lets it go.

"We have our monthly meeting next week where we will be discussing our tactics and plans. The Lib Dems may have seen a drop in their popularity due to joining the Conservatives in the Coalition Government, but, since the Brexit vote, our membership locally has risen sharply. Lots of younger people are looking for a clear voice, an unambiguous voice on the issues raised during the referendum campaign. In this constituency the majority voted to Remain and many of those Remain voters were young people. They are now wishing to put their energy into making sure that any Brexit deal is not going to harm them or their causes. I've learned a long time ago that young people's energies need to be harnessed and, hopefully, some of them will wish to be candidates at next year's council elections and, what's more, they'll be excellent too."

"Let's get back to you as I can't really turn this profile into a Party Political Broadcast for the Liberal Democrat Party."

"That's a shame. That reminds me, am I allowed to see the final copy before it goes to print?"

"I'll email you the first draft by tomorrow evening."

"Brilliant."

"Right then, I think I have probably enough for your profile. Just a couple of things. I'm curious about why you opted to
90

study and teach planning and the other thing is, sorry, this may seem a bit intrusive, but you and Gavin have no children. Is there…?"

"The last question is easy to answer. We couldn't have children. The first one is harder. I have always been interested in geography, in other cultures and travelling. Probably thanks to Celie. When I started my degree in geography, I had no idea I would end up being an expert in planning. Planning was a module that happened to be taught by a really gorgeous guy. There you are, that's my skeleton!"

"You took planning as a module because you fancied the lecturer!"

"Sounds awful, the way you put it. It's far more complicated than that but you want to give your readers a laugh, go ahead."

"Well, thanks, I think that's it then. See you at the next Council meeting."

"Yes, you will."

Both Chris and Beth walk towards the front door. As Beth is about to let Chris out, he turns. "Off the record, what do you think of the supermarket plan?"

Beth smiles sweetly. "I haven't read the details yet but you'll find out next week, like everyone else." With that she opens the door. "Thanks for profiling me."

With Chris gone she slumps on the sofa. She is cross with herself for having failed to say things about the refugees and about the ongoing crisis in her own life regarding Brexit. She realises Chris never asked her about these things. Maybe he was warned not to.

Chapter 18 – Intolerant

Donald Trump is the winner of the Presidential Election in the United States. Beth hears the news on the radio first thing in the morning. At hearing the Brexit outcome, she had collapsed and cried all day. The Trump news leaves her blank; she had been expecting it. To Beth the world has gone mad and she is genuinely concerned about her own sanity but in a different way. She has never understood selfishness, never felt an anti-foreigner feeling in her heart, never desired for her own country to be greater than another.

"You've seen the news?" Gavin walks into the kitchen from the living room.

"I've just heard it on the radio. Hearing that guy's voice is quite enough for me; I really don't want to see his face as well."

"You're not going to scream?" Gavin is looking quite anxiously at Beth.

"Right now, I'm beyond screaming. I just feel thoroughly depressed."

"Cheer up; maybe he won't turn out to be as bad as...."

"Shut up Gavin, I may not feel like screaming at the radio but I can easily scream at you if you try and defend this arsehole for just one second." Beth gives Gavin a look that cuts him to the core.

"Do you mind!" Gavin looks Beth defiantly back in the eye and raises his voice. "I am entitled to an opinion you know. I don't always have to agree with my clever wife. Just because I am a farmer and she is a lecturer and a Councillor, doesn't mean to say I can't think for myself."

"Are you seriously going to stick up for an anti-Muslim, anti-Mexican, woman hating and grabbing, money spinning businessman who is threatening world peace?" Beth sounds incredulous.

"I am not going to defend all that crap. All I am saying is we must give the guy a chance to show what he can do to help Americans into work." Gavin is still shouting.

"My heart bleeds for the poor old Americans!" Beth is not sure whether to take Gavin seriously or not. It's as if she's married to a stranger. "Do you know, I'm off to work. I don't want to hear any more defence of Trump. If you're going to be a Trump supporter, I'm off!" She notices Gavin's eyes looking surprised.

"Yes, get off to work! It's more important than listening to your husband's arguments."

"My husband's indefensible comments! I'm off to work but if there's any more of that crap coming from you, I'm off for good! Get it?"

Beth scrambles for her stuff and roars out of the drive. She is really screaming now, behind the wheel, on the top of her voice. At the end of their long drive she pulls over in order to get a grip on herself. She has heard comments from Gavin about Brexit and now Trump that make her feel giddy with insecurity. She can see Anna standing in the window who has noticed her sitting in the car. Instinctively Beth picks up her phone and pretends to talk into it. Anna, she thinks, there's another one I don't trust but I ought to see her, keep up some sort of charade that nothing has changed.

The university is now Beth's haven. All the students and lecturers are talking about Trump and nobody is defending him. Trump is a hated man through and through. Beth relaxes amongst the anti-Trump rhetoric. She overhears one student say: "I don't want to hate but Trump is so intolerant of so many people and things I stand for, and I hate intolerance."

Yes, thinks Beth, that's just it. I hate intolerance. Does that make me hate intolerant people?

The day passes quickly and it's dark early. Beth dreads having to go home. She feels at home in the university, home she reckons is a place where you are supposed to be able to relax. Gavin will probably argue that it's a place where you can freely express your opinion. Beth feels that this opinion cannot include intolerance of somebody different whether an immigrant or a gay person.

She spots the student who spoke so eloquently earlier in a group of other students. They are discussing protests. Beth quietly joins them. Instead of a lecturer, she feels like a student. She's transported back to Belgium 30 years ago. One of the students recognises her. "You're Dr Beth Evans, aren't you?"

"I am."

"What do you think of the Trump victory?" he asks.

"Depressing!" Beth answers.

"Will you come along to the protest we're organising? Maybe you can be one of our speakers?" It's the eloquent young female student.

"I'll think about it. Are you setting up a Facebook group? Send me a link." She gets up.

The female student follows her. "Hi, I was in the audience when you spoke at the Refugees Need Our Help meeting. I think you're awesome."

"What's your name?" They walk and talk towards the car park.

"Naomi."

"What are you studying?"

"Computer science. I'm in my second year."

"How are you finding student life?"

"It's great. I just love my independence."

"Well, Naomi, it's been lovely meeting you. This is my car. I need to go home." Beth smiles at Naomi but Naomi is perceptive.

"You look tired. Did you stay up all night to watch the results?"

"No, those days are over for me. I need my sleep." She laughs but then looks at Naomi and is serious. "I am feeling depressed over Trump's victory. Could 2016 really have got worse?"

"Yeh, it's been a right shit year, hasn't it. First Brexit and now Trump. Perhaps you'd like to meet up for a cuppa one day?"

Beth struggles to keep the tears at bay. Nobody has asked her to come along for a cuppa for such a long time. She breaks into a smile. "I would love that!"

"Ok, are Wednesdays good for you?"

"Yes, Wednesdays are the best. How about next week?"

"Great, you know that little cafe near the seafront, in that side street leading to the Glan-y-Môr? It's called Chez Nous."

"I know it. Shall we say eleven? I realise you students aren't great earlier than that."

"Eleven is lovely, see you then."

Beth watches Naomi from the car. Naomi lithely runs up the steps back into the building. What it is to be young and independent! And now, home, she thinks, whatever home is. This time there is no stopping the tears.

The drive back to the farm is over all too quickly for Beth's liking. She dreads another confrontation with Gavin.

The light in the large shed is on but the house is hulled in darkness. The honking of geese is clearly heard as Beth steps out. She dumps her stuff in the house and puts on her wellies.

"Why are you still with the geese?"

Gavin turns to face her. "Oh, hello darling."

"Is there a problem? I'm sure I left the feeders and water ok this morning."

"No problem. It's ok Beth. I was just wondering if I could slaughter some early and put them in the freezer rather than do the whole lot in one go. So I've been checking their weights."

"Why?" Beth is genuinely surprised.

"I'll need this shed for Gwenith's sheep, won't I?"

"Not till after the geese have gone surely?"

"I just thought I might clear half of it next week so I can prepare it and it'll save you some work."

"I've always helped with the goose slaughter! And in any case,
96

we have the Young Farmers booked for the second weekend in December." Beth is struggling to keep her emotions under control. When she first moved to this farm it was she who suggested the goose side-line for the Christmas market. She set it up, created the demand, has fed and watered the geese throughout the months before Christmas; she has plucked hundreds of geese over the years and has made the finest Belgian pâté with the goose livers. Her order book for this year is full. Gavin is here undermining her. If it isn't Brexit, it's the farm they argue over. Beth makes an important decision. It's on the spot but it's all she feels she can do right there and then.

"I'm going in to see about supper. From now on you're responsible for the geese, for all of it. I'll leave the order book in the kitchen." She doesn't wait for an answer; she marches out of the shed and across the yard. She's crying again, this time more out of frustration and anger than of sadness.

Gavin enters ten minutes later. He is smiling sheepishly. "There's a casserole in the oven."

"I've noticed." Beth is laying the table.

"Don't you want to sit in the living room?"

"You can; I'm sitting here." Beth's demeanour is cold.

"Oh, come on Beth, I was trying to be organised. Can't I ever do anything right!"

"You didn't consult me. The geese are really mine, well, it's my part of this business and you, you, you just make a decision. How do you expect me to react?" Beth's voice is cracking.

"Ok, I won't do it! I'll stick with the original plan. Have it your way!" Gavin disappears into the bathroom.

Beth dishes up the food and eats in silence. Gavin joins her at the table but scowls the whole way through dinner.

"That was very nice, thanks." Beth is speaking with exaggerated politeness.

"Oh good." Gavin is not coping with Beth's quietness. He really prefers her shouting. He realises he is in the wrong and decides to make amends.

"You know that garden in Anglesey you wanted to go and visit?"

"Yeh, what about it?"

"I thought we could go this weekend, you know, just you and me."

"What do you want from me?" Beth is not taken in.

"I just think we need a weekend away together. I'll book us a B&B or a hotel."

"You book a hotel!"

"No need to be so sarky. I'm quite capable of making a phone call, you know."

"And who's going to look after the farm?"

"I'll ask Owen. He and Gwenith owe us one. What about it?"

Beth melts. "Ok, I haven't got anything that can't wait."

"Brilliant!" Gavin gets up and takes the plates to the sink.

"Cup of tea?"

"Yes please."

98

Chapter 19 – Scared

The church hall of St Michael's is packed for a change. Beth counts at least fifty people. There are some new faces and some she hasn't seen for a few years. They are all looking excited.

Beth finds a seat next to a lady she doesn't recognise. "Hi, I'm Beth Evans. Welcome."

"Thank you. I recognise you. You're a Councillor, aren't you?"

"That's right. So what brought you out tonight? The weather is pretty foul, isn't it?"

"I think the Lib Dems have such a good chance of winning in Richmond. I thought it was about time I helped to make it happen, get that Tory lot out."

"Good for you."

The Chair taps on the table and the room quietens but a sense of enthusiasm hangs like a hum above them all.

After a warm welcome and a short meeting to deal with business, they break for tea. Councillor Bryn Jones walks over to Beth who is busy in conversation with some new people. "Beth, have you got a moment?"

"Of course. Excuse me please." Beth turns away from the newcomers and faces Bryn. "Hi Bryn, what can I do?"

"Have you had a look at those supermarket plans yet?"

"Yes, I have."

"So, what do you make of them? You were awfully quiet last week. Normally you have so much to say."

"Bryn, I have had a lot on my plate just lately. I realise you were all counting on me but, you know, one more week won't matter. I'll speak at tomorrow's meeting."

"Oh, thanks Beth, I just wanted to make sure you're ok. I just got the feeling that something wasn't quite right."

Beth smiles but in her heart she doesn't feel like smiling at all. "Thanks for the concern. I hope this by-election is going to put the Brexiteers on the back foot. Any hope for a decent compromise will make me feel better."

Bryn gawps at her uncomprehendingly. "I thought you were ill!"

"I can't say I've been feeling great but I'm not ill. Life has just been a bit of a bugger really but look at all these people tonight." Beth gazes around, this time with a genuine look of delight on her face. "They all want the Lib Dems to win Richmond on behalf of the Remainers. It gives you some faith back, don't you think?" Beth looks directly at Bryn.

He shuffles his feet and stares at the ground. "Trouble is, the people have voted Brexit and we need to honour it." Bryn says these words like a mantra.

Beth has heard it so many times on the news, she is sick of it. "What are you actually trying to say Bryn?" The words come out more strident than she had intended but this anger that she is constantly trying to suppress in public since June is rising of its own volition.

The newcomers who are still standing nearby stop talking and look in their direction.

"Not now Beth," says Bryn.

Beth makes a rapid decision. "Ok Bryn, not now, not here

over tea. I'll bring it up in ten minutes when we're all seated and we'll have this out in front of everybody." With that she turns her back on Bryn and continues with the conversation in the group of newcomers.

Beth is watching Bryn across the table from her. She is scribbling away on her notepad but peers over every few seconds. Bryn looks nervous.

The Chair again welcomes everybody and the meeting gets under way again. Beth raises her hand. Outwardly she calmly awaits her turn; inwardly she is rehearsing the words over and over again and is barely conscious of what other people are saying.

"Yes, Beth."

"Thank you Chair. I am also delighted at the massive turnout this evening and pleased that so many people are willing to go to London for a weekend door-knocking in Richmond. What I wish to have debated here tonight is our stance on Brexit and see if we can agree what our local stance should be, the same as the national party, the same as the Welsh party, more nuanced to reflect local conditions, and how our local stance can be used to marshal support for the local elections next year."

"Thank you Beth. I have to say I'm a bit bemused by your question as I thought the Lib Dem stance was absolutely clear." The Chair looks genuinely perplexed.

Beth carries on. "I happen to think that, although I myself fully support the stance as so eloquently outlined by our leader, that there are members of our local party who feel quite differently and I think we need to have this debate."

The Chair looks around. A number of hands have gone up. Bryn's hand stays down. Beth looks him expectantly in the eye. The Chair follows her eye. He looks back at Beth and notices her set jaw. He allows people to speak. Several newcomers express themselves passionately in favour of Remain and explain that this is the reason they're here. He turns to Bryn Jones.

"Bryn, you've been a Councillor here now for some twenty years. You know our electorate pretty well I should say. What do you think?"

Bryn is a highly respected Councillor. He is a local farmer and has been President of the National Farmers Union before becoming a Councillor. He is also a Governor of his local school. He's a true stalwart of the local community. He has lived here all his life. His opinion matters. When he opens his mouth everyone listens quietly. "I hear what you're all saying and I agree that we should have a strategy for getting the best deal but, actually, the Richmond by-election is about the expansion of Heathrow airport. That's what Zac Goldsmith has resigned over. We've had the Referendum and the people of this country have spoken." Bryn is beginning to sound like a stuck record again, thinks Beth. "I believe in democracy. We are the Liberal Democrats after all. We have to accept the outcome of the Referendum. We're not going to have a second one."

A woman sitting about ten seats away from Beth doesn't put her hand up but shouts, "So, what are you saying, we should just lie down and take it!"

The Chair tries to stop her talking but before he manages to speak there are at least fifteen people talking and shouting at once. Beth looks at Bryn and he returns her gaze this time.

Order returns. The Chair is smiling but he is red in the face. "Beth, you wish to come back on what Bryn has said."

"Thank you Chair. Yes, I want to thank Bryn for his honesty. I

102

have to say though that you sound just like James Coburn. I'd like to think that in this constituency, which voted by a reasonable margin to Remain, that we can be true to our electorate and stick up for them, stick up for the 48% in the country who voted Remain and also fight for the plight of our local farmers."

Bryn shakes his head. "Most of our farmers voted Brexit! I've spoken to lots of them last summer prior to the Referendum. You may well think that Brexit is bad for farmers but many of them are sick of form filling and sick of the bureaucracy. They couldn't wait to get out of the EU."

Beth notices Bryn look at her and she is aware that his eyes are actually full of pity. She is suddenly scared. A terrible thought forms in her brain. It's scarier than the red balloon experience. She squashes it determinedly with logic. Even so, she's glad when the Chair puts a motion on the issue to a vote and it goes overwhelmingly her way.

Driving home that night she recalls her meeting with James Coburn and how she had called him a traitor. It was behind his back. What should she call Bryn? She has always got on so well with him.

The scary thought creeps back into her brain. She has to stop the car as she feels herself starting to hyperventilate. She is only a mile from home. Bryn's sympathetic eyes keep popping in front of her face. No, no, no, she tells herself. I'm just imagining it. She wills herself to calm down and drives slowly home.

Gavin greets her cheerfully when she enters. "Hello Cariad, how was the meeting?"

Chapter 20 – Needy

"This really is a cosy cafe, isn't it? I've seen it from the outside but I haven't set foot in it since they've done it up."

"Glad you like it. When we had Fresher's Week, we were taken on a cafe tour. Chez Nous was my favourite then and it still is."

"Well, you've only been here a year. Hopefully, you'll find a few more to your taste. Come on, what are you drinking?"

"I asked you to come for a coffee," Naomi protests politely.

"Lecturers earn, students just owe. Tell me what you fancy. Oh, and a cake as well. I feel like we both deserve a treat."

Five minutes later Beth and Naomi are tucking into a delicious home-baked slice of cake and enjoying their coffee and chatting as if they've known each other for years. Beth actually feels ridiculously young as if she's a student again. Naomi is so easy going, her manners are mature and she talks about politics in a knowledgeable fashion. Beth's curious about her.

"You sound as if you've been a member of a political party all of your life," she says.

"In a manner of speaking I suppose I have," laughs Naomi. "My mother took me in the pushchair to protests in London and I got taken to conferences every year, sometimes twice a year."

"Sounds like an interesting childhood."

"I had a marvellous time. Both my mum and dad are members of the Green Party. Sorry, I realise you're a Lib Dem."

"Oh, don't apologise." Beth hopes Naomi carries on. Her mannerism is infectious. It cheers her up.

"Oh, well, in any case, they always discussed things, anything, at home and talked them through with me and my older brother."

"Sounds wonderful!"

"They taught us to argue, to stick up for people who can't stick up for themselves, to stick up for animals, you name it. That's why I immediately joined the Refugees Need Our Help group. I've also set up a Young Green group at the Uni. And now we've got to fight this Trump bum!" Naomi has fire in her eyes.

"It's never ending." Beth's remark comes out with a sigh.

Naomi puts down her fork and looks Beth calmly in the eye. "You really are very tired, aren't you?"

"Is it that obvious?"

"Well, I don't think it's that obvious, unless you're looking for it."

"Why would you be looking for it?" Beth is shocked and surprised.

"I told you I'm a computer scientist student. I heard you speak at the Refugees meeting and I've read your profile in the Herald. I checked out your Facebook page. I also managed to dig a bit deeper and I know you've had to deal with a load of shit."

Beth is quiet. The tears start to well up. She is overwhelmed by Naomi's kind-heartedness. Her brain feels crowded with emotions and questions. Naomi allows her the space she needs.

"Naomi, you realise that if I had had children, mine would be your age. I suppose if I had had a daughter like you, she'd be my best friend."

"My mother is my best friend," Naomi says confidently, "But I have lots of other friends and so does my mother. Our house was always overflowing with people and we learned to get on with people of all ages. I have friends who are in their 60s, 70s and even 80s. I'm happy to be your friend."

"Thank you Naomi. It means a lot to me." Beth is searching her brain for people she's called friends over the years: Christine at work, but she's friends on a purely professional level; Bryn, well, she's not sure how she feels about him now; Rhian from the Gardening Club can get stuffed as far as she's concerned; Gwenith has never liked her – her smiles and interests in Beth are just skin deep; Sophia, oh yes, she was really friendly with her but as her tutor not as an equal; and then there's Anna – she feels let down by her and she knows why, the answer is obvious.

"Naomi," she starts cautiously, "I've been friends with my work for the last 30 years. I've put my all into the university and into my Council work and into the Gardening Club. I've worked my socks off on the farm and I've worked my socks off for this country. I thought I had friends. I realise now that all these people were just colleagues. I haven't had a conversation like this with anybody for years. And I don't even know you!" She stares across the table at Naomi who is patiently waiting for her to go on. "It's weird as I feel as if I've known you for years."

Naomi gently takes her hand. "Would you like another coffee? Or perhaps something else, a camomile tea or a fruity tea?"

"Thank you Naomi. I've never been one to drink fruit tea but perhaps I should give it a go."

"You won't believe the choices here. They have special tea for women."

"Really!"

"Let me surprise you." Naomi leaves the table, leaves Beth in her sad thoughts.

Beth looks around the little cafe properly for the first time that morning. She recognises a few faces but there's no-one she knows by name. She feels safer in this anonymity. Nobody is trying to attract her attention either. She sighs a grateful sigh.

Naomi returns with two tall mugs. Beth looks at the label. 'Tea for Women's Health'. "Thank you Naomi."

The tea is extremely hot but Beth is determined to sip it immediately to gain from its miraculous strength-giving powers. She accepts that it's all likely to be in her head but is willing to try anything at the moment in order to sort her confused head. The tea tastes surprisingly nice. "Mmm, I actually like this." Beth's smiling.

"You know I said I checked out your Facebook page?" Naomi begins.

"Yes, Facebook, what a nightmare," Beth responds despondently.

"Did you ever notice some people posting messages of support though?" Naomi is undeterred.

"I couldn't bear to look for a while. Not after Jo Cox's death. I put on some stringent blocks, at least that's what I think I did, and then after August for a while I only looked at family stuff. I only have a very small family so there's not much to look at."

"How about your twitter account?"

"What about it?"

"Do you still use it? I haven't noticed you tweeting at all."

"When I got so many hate messages, I tried to avoid all unnecessary social media stuff. The worst threats were on my mobile phone. As a Councillor all your details go online, in case somebody needs your help. All I got was abuse." Beth sips some more of her tea. "This tea is lovely. Thanks. I never knew this sort of tea would be so delicious." She's wanting to change the subject as the images of abuse she's received are getting too strong for her. Naomi won't let her.

"What did you do with all the messages and tweets?"

"Gavin, that's my husband, deleted them all for me one evening."

"Did you go to the police?"

"No!"

"Why not?"

Beth is wondering why she's allowing herself to be questioned by this young student. She actually doesn't have the answer, or she's afraid of giving it. She hesitates longer than she intends. Naomi says, "Sorry, I'm being totally impertinent."

"Actually, I think you've been really helpful." Beth's found her voice. "This morning, this cuppa, it's been great. It's done me the world of good. Thank you again Naomi."

"Beth, if you really think so, we should do it again but, if you don't mind me saying so, and I'm so sorry but I have to bring my mother into the conversation again, but she is a counsellor you see, a counsellor who helps people."

"Yeh, I get it."

"Perhaps you should see a counsellor to help you get over these awful experiences. I read what those dreadful people wrote on your Facebook page, sorry but they are definitely not all deleted, and can only guess at the nature of your phone messages. Anybody would struggle with that."

"Thank you Naomi, you really are very thoughtful. I'll think about it."

"Phew, no umbrage."

"God, no!" Beth really is laughing now.

"Maybe I can be your friend on Facebook. I can help with comments that chase the nasties away for you."

"Ok, send me a request!"

"I will. Look out for NeedToKnowMe, that's me."

"That's a great name!"

On the way home Beth thinks about Naomi's suggestion of visiting a counsellor. What have I got to lose?

Chapter 21 – Moody

"The Lib Dems have won!"

"In Richmond? They've done it?" Beth jumps out of bed.

"Steady on Beth."

"What's to steady on? Gavin, that's great news! Thanks for the tea by the way. Let me turn the telly on."

The morning goes by in a flash. Beth is finding herself smile most of the time. Her lectures are great and her students clearly appreciate them. The weekly shop at the supermarket is even plain-sailing and some people stop to talk to her, congratulating her on the Lib Dem victory. It feels like old times.

The whole day has given Beth the confidence to start looking at her Facebook page again and to tweet a happy tweet. She thinks carefully about the message she wishes to convey. When she gets home she jots down, 'The Lib Dems have won and their stance on Brexit was clear. The 48% who voted Remain are not a bunch of losers but nearly half the country who cannot and should not be ignored, not ridden over roughshod. That doesn't mean to say the 48% will try to overturn what the 52% voted for but perhaps a decent compromise can be reached.'

"Ok, here goes, how do I put that into 140 characters?"

"Hello Cariad, how do you put what into 140 characters?"

"Hi darling. I thought I might send a tweet."

"You must have had a good day."

"You too, you called me Cariad."

"Hey, that's not so unusual! Actually Beth, I have had rather a difficult day." Gavin sounds serious.

"Oh?" Beth looks up from her phone. She sees Gavin properly.

"Bird flu has broken out. Looks like we've got to get all the birds indoors."

"Oh shit!" Beth puts the phone down and for the first time that day her smile disappears. "What do you know for sure?"

"Well, so far it's been found in East England but precautionary measures have been put into place. 'Keep all poultry away from wild birds'."

Beth gets up and hugs Gavin. "Hey, our geese are all going to be slaughtered next weekend in any case."

"Yeh, and then we're going to have to bring the chickens into the shed just when we're going to have the lambs in."

"There's only about twenty of them now; they just need a small corner. In any case, maybe it's all a bit of hot air and it'll blow over soon. Where did you hear the news?"

"It was on the news, on the telly."

"Have you checked the Welsh Government's website?"

"I haven't got round to it yet!"

"Gavin, you look exhausted. Go and have a bath. I'll cook us something and check the website out."

"I just need to go and see Anna."

"You need what!" Beth is truly surprised.

"Anna phoned earlier. One of her pigs isn't looking too great. Could I pop over and have a look, just to reassure her that she doesn't need to call the vet. I said I would."

"That's really nice of you Gavin." Beth gives him another hug and kisses him. "Better have a quick shower then, hadn't you. Give Anna my love."

Beth dives into the freezer. She's determined to stay on top, not to let anything get her down. Gavin has been calling her Cariad again quite often, just like he used to. They also had a wonderful weekend in Anglesey. The Lib Dems have won. Things will get better again. What's a bit of bird flu? She digs amongst the frozen apples and runner beans till she finds a couple of pots of curry. "That'll do! My favourite quick meal!"

The rice goes on, the curry goes in the microwave and Beth is on her phone again. "First things first, Facebook!"

Beth takes a gulp of air as she opens her page. She laughs though as she sees a very funny post from NeedToKnowMe who is congratulating the Lib Dems on their win. Beth replies straightaway. She copies almost word for word the words she noted earlier. Then she tweets, '48% # will not be pushed around by 52%. Compromise please! Hard Brexit will be damaging to 100%'

Gavin is out of the shower before the rice is cooked. "Shall I pop over now or after dinner?"

"I'll be dishing up in two minutes. I'll come with you after dinner. I should say hi in any case."

Beth's phone makes lots of noises as they eat the curry but she ignores them all. Right now her priorities are Gavin, bird flu, Anna and a sick pig. "Have you had a good look at our own chickens and geese?"

"Of course I have. Can't see anything the matter with them."

"Good, let's hope it stays that way."

"The starlings can still get in by the roof vents."

"Do starlings carry bird flu?"

"I think all birds can but some are more susceptible."

"Like what?"

"Ducks, geese, swans."

"Oh well, I'll have a good read on the Government's website and see what they advise."

"Lovely curry by the way."

"It's one of yours, it has lamb in it."

"If we have to slaughter early, you'll have a freezer full of goose curry." Gavin has a cheeky grin on his face but Beth's not fooled. She knows Gavin is worried. He doesn't handle disease well, too many awful memories of the horrific foot and mouth outbreak.

"You'll have to feed all those runner beans to Anna's pigs first in order to make space. Come on, let's go. I hate these dark nights."

Beth remains cheerful even though they leap from one puddle to the next in the rutted lane.

"Anna, hi," Beth shouts from the back door.

"Hello Beth, how lovely of you to come over. Come in quick, it's horrid out there."

"Gavin has gone to check that pig of yours. I thought I'd tag along."

"You're looking cheerful."

"I am. I've been in a jolly mood all day since I heard about the Lib Dem victory in Richmond."

"Would you like a cup of tea?"

"That would be wonderful."

"I'll make a pot. Will Gavin have time for one?"

"I'm sure he will. I don't think he'll be long."

The back door opens. "No, that didn't take long."

"You were incredibly quick. What do you think? Do I need to call the vet?"

"That depends."

"Oh!" Anna looks alarmed.

"Did I hear you say tea?"

"Yes, I've just put it in the pot. Let's go into the living room and I'll pour it out."

"So, have you changed your feeding routine in the last few days or given the pigs something new?" Gavin catches Beth's eye who struggles not to burst out laughing.

"I gave them all the apples from the store room. I really didn't feel up to doing something with them this year. I suppose some were going a bit off."

"Well, that's probably the answer then. They're just scouring a little. You'll need to call the vet if they don't improve in the next few days. But I don't think you need to worry."

"Unlike us, there's an outbreak of bird flu."

"Is there? Where's that come from?" Anna sounds panicked.

"It started in Europe and now it's in East Anglia," Gavin states.

"These things always start in Europe. Same as Dutch elm disease and ash die-back." Anna is beginning to get het up.

"Hang on a second Anna, the bird flu is in the wild population of birds. They come here to spend the winter." Gavin is a bit nonplussed over Anna's reaction. Beth is biting her tongue. Gavin carries on. "And the countries in Europe where they've found it, like The Netherlands, have clamped down immediately to stop the spread."

"So it's Europe that's telling us what to do then." Anna continues to make her case.

"Actually, it's up to the Welsh Government to tell us what to do," Gavin argues back.

"Well, I bet they'll just do as they're told by Europe and...."

Before Anna can finish her sentence Beth has got up and put her cup down. "Thanks for the tea Anna, I'll be seeing you. Come on Gavin, we have lots to do." With that she marches for the door.

"Sorry Anna, I think you've touched a raw nerve," Gavin says. He gulps his tea down. "I'd better go after her."

Anna is left with her mouth wide open as Gavin shuts the back door. He catches up with Beth by their own back door.

"What you go storming out like that for?"

"What d'you think?" Beth takes off her coat and boots and slams the kettle on. "I've listened to her for years going on about Europe and argued nicely, I've explained in detail how it all works. She's so bloody ignorant! She's been asking me the same questions over and over again and I've spent ages telling her what responsibilities the Welsh Government has, where laws are made, who makes what laws," Beth draws breath in the middle of her tirade against Anna, "I am so sick of her Gavin!" Beth is close to tears now. "Do you realise she knows how this anti-Europe stuff upsets me."

"How?"

"She's actually largely avoided the subject since the Brexit vote. But she saw me happy today and probably thought she could start up again!"

"Beth, that's ridiculous! I don't think she's that clever. Go on, sit down, I'll finish the tea."

"What really gets me is that she's always telling me how wonderful I am." Beth puts the accent on I. "But as far as she's concerned all foreigners suck. I am the exception. And the irony is that I am probably the only foreigner she knows!"

"She reads the wrong paper."

"I'm well aware of that." Beth sips her tea and stares into space. Her happy day has turned sour.

Gavin puts his arm around her. "Come on, don't let Anna spoil your day. Forget about the bird flu too. I'll check the website tomorrow. Shall we watch a film?"

"Don't know if I'm in the mood now. I'll go and check on the chickens and the geese. Maybe I'll have an early night."

116

"I'll find us a comedy. In any case, the chickens are in their house. You can't see a thing in there. Go on Beth, relax, I want to see you smile."

"Ok then, I'll tell you one thing though, I shan't see Anna any more. She can get stuffed."

"Beth, you're just being ridiculous! You have to get over this bloody Brexit thing. Do you want to lose all your friends?"

"Like who? Why should I be friends with anybody who voted Brexit? People who voted Brexit obviously don't care about the likes of me so why should I be friends with them?"

"I keep telling you that not everybody voted Brexit for anti-immigrant reasons!"

"Is that what they tell you in the pub on your darts night?" Beth raises her voice.

"Some, and others don't!"

"Yeh, like Martin; he clearly hates foreigners. Is he sucking up to you now?"

"I just try to get on with everybody, no matter how they voted."

"Well, sorry if I feel differently. You might think I'm touchy but there you have it. I don't want to watch a film. All I want to do is go to bed. My evening has been completely spoiled."

"Well, you can go on your own!"

Beth looks at Gavin. He has clearly had enough of her behaviour. Bryn's sympathetic eyes jump in front of her own. Her fear turns into anger. "Good, I will, enjoy the spare bedroom. It probably suits you better!"

Chapter 22 – Reckless

The next morning Beth is cross with herself for losing it with Gavin. She takes him tea in bed and gets on with the business of feeding the geese and chickens. After breakfast she checks her twitter account. Gavin creeps in. He looks over her shoulder to examine her screen.

"How many responses did you get to that tweet last night?" Gavin sounds incredulous.

"Thousands! Many very nice and plenty of crap like, 'get a life loser' or 'piss off if you don't like it here'. I know it's a daft free for all really. I don't think I'll bother again."

"Seems sensible to me. What are you up to today?"

"Checking the website for bird flu regulations, go into Uni, meet Naomi for a cuppa."

"Who's Naomi?"

"A computer science student. She's lovely."

"You're meeting up with a single student? Don't you think that could come across as really weird?" Gavin looks at Beth in a challenging way.

"I, I, she's not on my course. She's a fellow campaigner, that's all." Beth sounds flustered.

Gavin's not fooled. "You've always been friendly with your students but you've always also drawn a firm line. So, what's changed?"

Beth is quiet. She finds it hard to put into words to Gavin without upsetting him. He is obviously touchy at the moment and she realises she's been impatient with him. She's met up once more with Naomi. It's Naomi who's giving Beth some sort of confidence back, confidence to do what though? Walk out on Anna; yell at Gavin? She doesn't feel entirely comfortable with seeing a student herself either, not in this manner.

"Well?"

"Well, you must have realised that I've not been myself since the Brexit vote. I'm all over the place emotionally really. Naomi is helping me to put my thoughts into some sort of order."

Gavin barks sarcastically, "She's a bloody student, not a counsellor for god's sake!"

"I know." Beth's voice stays low. "In fact, her mother is a counsellor and Naomi has urged me to see one myself."

"Well, I think that is a bloody good idea." Gavin walks out of the kitchen and shuts the door loudly.

"Maybe it's marriage guidance counselling that's needed," Beth shouts after him. Gavin is out of earshot.

Beth has a lovely time in the cafe with Naomi. She tells Naomi about her arguments with Anna but refrains from revealing her feelings towards Gavin, how she switches from total devotion to complete frustration and even fearful distrust. Naomi listens intently. It's pretty clear to Beth that she ought to find a professional counsellor so she can discuss all her problems and it also doesn't appear fair to offload onto this young, albeit very capable, woman.

In her office she googles for private counsellors, dials a few numbers and actually makes an appointment. It's for real; Beth will see somebody to help her cope, someone in the next major city whose name she doesn't recognise, someone who, hopefully, won't know her either; it's for the following week.

"I've made an appointment," Beth declares when she gets home.

"An appointment for what?" Gavin sounds snappy.

"For us to see a marriage guidance counsellor," Beth smiles and immediately regrets joking about it. Gavin is clearly not in a good mood. He doesn't notice Beth's tone of voice, isn't watching her face either. Her words are sinking in though. He closes his laptop slowly and gets up. "You've done what!"

"I've made an appointment to see a counsellor. It's only for me. You did say you thought I ought to see one." Beth is feeling remarkably calm as she explores Gavin's angry features.

"You just said!"

"Yeh, I know what I just said. I was trying to make a joke. Sorry, I shouldn't make jokes about inappropriate topics. I'm trying to make light of a serious situation. I've never seen a counsellor in my life, not even." Beth stops abruptly.

"Yeh, sorry," Gavin begins, "Shall I cook dinner?"

Gavin's default position when he feels he's overstepped the mark, cook dinner and all will be ok again. Beth muses that perhaps she meant to say it, perhaps it isn't her, perhaps it is her marriage that's failing. But no, she thinks, it's been since Brexit that I've been feeling like this, sure? Sure; the word echoes round her brain. She doesn't feel sure of anything anymore.

After dinner Beth checks the geese and reassures herself that none of them are ill. She manages to smile at her healthy looking flock, knowing that soon they'll be turned into Christmas dinners. She ponders on the fragility of life, the shortness of it, the uncertainty of things.

"I'm off to darts, ok?"

"Yeh, fine," Beth replies absentmindedly.

"You're going to the Gardening Club?"

"No, I really can't be doing with it any longer. I've texted Rhian my apologies. Don't think she's bothered. You go and enjoy yourself. I'll probably be in bed when you get home."

"Alright, see you later." Gavin is still behaving awkwardly. Perhaps he too feels that it's not just Brexit that's the problem for Beth.

Beth turns on the telly and curls up on the sofa with a glass of wine. Her mind is wondering again over life and uncertainties. The stupid words 'the only thing in life that's certain is death and taxes' keep playing in her head over and over again. She imagines the words in Flemish and in French. They don't have the same impact in either language. She can't find anything on the telly to take her mind off the situation. She turns her laptop on and looks for the email she has had from the counsellor. She ignores all other stuff.

The counsellor has recommended that she writes a list of all the things that are bothering her plus a list of things about herself, well, two lists in fact, one positive, one negative. Beth grabs a piece of paper. She starts on the first list. It's easier than she had anticipated now that the pen is in her hand. 'Brexit, losing friends, not being supported by my husband, nasty tweets and Facebook messages, feeling lost, losing whatever identity I thought I had.' The words are just flowing out of her. 'Constant arguments with my husband, not feeling supported by fellow Remain campaigners, not knowing what's going to happen to my rights, not even sure if I'm able to stay here, not even sure if I want to stay here, where will I feel at home.' She breaks down. The actuality of putting her words onto paper for herself and this counsellor, this confidante, is making her face the total truth. Speaking in front of an audience or writing in the Herald was different; she didn't mention her husband there. That leads her to consider why, over and above his lack of support, he is bothering her so much. The pen flies to the paper. 'Gwenith, her sheep, the way Gavin goes out of his way to help Gwenith but he got so cross over Anna's pigs.' "Poor counsellor!" she exclaims out loud.

Beth pours herself another glass of wine. She decides to put the rest of it in the cellar; she doesn't want Gavin to find her comatose. She tackles the list of positives and negatives.

'Positives: good lecturer; conscientious councillor; good goose keeper; excellent pâté maker; ok gardener; positive committee member; caring neighbour; kind daughter; brilliant linguist. Negatives: don't like to be criticised; don't like insecurity; argumentative wife; don't make friends easily.'

"I'm nothing but a bloody show-off," she shouts out loud, "No wonder people don't want to be friends with me!" She quietly reflects upon her past. She thinks, I was such a party girl when I was younger. What has happened to me? Nothing can hold back the tears, the negative thoughts, the utter loneliness.

Beth gets up, goes back to the cellar and fills her glass to the brim. She downs the glass in the living room, grabs the pen and writes under the negatives, 'likes to get plastered'. She screws up all the bits of paper and throws them on the fire. Her laptop is going in and out of focus. She shuts it and stumbles up the stairs. Beth doesn't care if Gavin finds her comatose; she doesn't care about anything.

Chapter 23 – Hurting

"Come in, please take a seat. Beth, isn't it?"

"Thanks Samara." Beth sits on the edge of the comfortable chair. She feels on edge, and on the edge of her comfort zone, on the edge of a big change in her life.

"Call me Sam please." Samara takes a pen and a notepad. "Beth, many people benefit enormously from counselling. The ones who benefit the most are the people who are open and honest."

Beth nods.

Samara continues. "I sent you some material through, the ground rules. Did you read them?"

Beth nods again.

"Do you have any questions about them?"

"No, thanks, they're clear," Beth manages to whisper.

"Ok then. I suggested that you make a couple of lists, one of the things that are bothering you and one of the positive and negative things you think about yourself. Did you have a chance to write these down?" Samara keeps her calm smile through saying this.

"I did write it all down but then I threw them into the fire." Beth is suddenly feeling her argumentative side coming to the fore. She shifts in her seat and relaxes a bit. Samara makes a few notes.

"Perhaps you can recall what you wrote down and why you burned them afterwards."

"I got cross and then drunk."

"Do you think you have a drink problem?"

"No, I don't! I just sometimes need to blot out everything."

"What things do you feel the need to blot out?"

"Brexit, bloody Brexit! And my husband, when he's, I don't know," Beth is letting go, "When he's not caring about me or the things I care about and, and, I don't seem to have any friends, and…." Tears are gushing down Beth's cheeks. She blurts through them: "I just feel so bloody lonely."

Samara hands Beth a couple of tissues from a box on the table. While Beth blows her nose, Samara does a bit more scribbling.

"Ok Beth, you're clearly feeling very down and on your own at the moment. I just need to ask you if you have been to see your GP at all, if you are taking any anti-depressants."

"No, I haven't, I don't want anything."

"That's ok. You've done the right thing to come for help. It's very hard to find answers on your own. The answer certainly won't be at the bottom of a glass." Samara doesn't sound preachy, just sympathetic.

Beth pulls herself together, wipes her eyes.

"Ok Beth, I guess some of those things were on your lists."

"Yeh."

"Can we write the list together now? Shall we start with the things that are bothering you?"

"Ok."

"I'll write them down."

124

"No chance of them being burned then." Beth manages a smile.

"In your email you wrote you're from Belgium originally. That's correct?"

"Yes."

"Ok, just checking. When you're ready. Tell me everything that's bothering you."

"Brexit, losing friends because of it, not being supported by Gavin."

"Gavin?"

"That's my husband. Feeling alone, not knowing who I am any more, not feeling welcome."

"Not feeling welcome where?"

"In this country, in Wales, in the UK."

"Ok, carry on."

"I feel insecure. I've had to put up with a load of shit on Facebook and Twitter, I've had death threats, told to bugger off where I came from, called the Bloody Belgian Bitch, you can Google that now and it leads to me."

"Have you been to the police about that?"

"No, in all fairness to Gavin, he did delete a load of this stuff but it has stopped me from doing all the things I was used to doing on social media before." Beth starts to cry afresh and needs more tissues.

"Ok Beth, I think some of these things need unpicking a bit. It sounds as if you've been overwhelmed these last few months and have been on an emotional roller coaster. No wonder you're feeling the way you are. I would like to suggest something."

"Ok." Beth sniffs.

"If you at the end of this session feel that coming here is helping you, I'd like you to have another go at home at writing a list of your positive and negative characteristics. The list of things that are bothering you I feel fall into two camps. Tell me if you agree with me. The first camp is the public's decision to vote for Brexit and the effect it's having on you personally as a Belgian citizen, the second one is the support you need from your husband, family and friends and your very real perception that this is lacking."

"Yeh, I guess so. It seems so trivial when you put it like that."

"Oh no Beth, this is not trivial. You are suffering!" Samara is speaking firmly.

Beth cries anew. When she dries her tears she says, "I've always been such a strong person. People have always relied on me and now, now, I feel I need to rely on others and they're not there."

Samara makes more notes. "Beth," she says when she looks up, "We have half an hour left. Can I suggest we have a chat about your marriage? Have you any idea why Gavin is not supporting you in the way you think he should? Let's start with your expectations of him."

"Simple," Beth says crossly, "Gavin never once came out to public meetings, help me out on a street stall, or write any letters of support."

"When was this exactly?"

"During the referendum campaign."

126

"Do you think Gavin was, like many people, perhaps not worried it was going to happen, did he perhaps think the British people would easily vote to Remain so he wasn't needed?"

"Perhaps, but, I struggle to put my finger on it, it's as if he didn't care."

"And what about since the referendum?"

"Well, as I said, he's helped to deal with the awful messages, but, apart from that, he just seems resigned to Brexit and wants me to do the same! He doesn't share my anxiety as a foreigner at all."

"What does Gavin do?"

"He's a farmer, we have a farm. He works on it full time and I do part of it."

"What else do you do?"

"I'm a full time lecturer and a Councillor, not one like you, I'm a County Councillor."

"Do you have family close by, children?"

"We couldn't have children." The pain in Beth's voice is palpable.

"I'm so sorry."

"My family is all in Belgium. I still have an elderly mother there. Gavin's parents both died a few years ago. He has a sister who's married with two children."

"Are you close?"

"Gavin is close to them but they've never been particularly

welcoming to me."

"What are you and Gavin like at home together? Do you argue over the housework or things like that? And, what about your sex life?"

"We never used to argue, not really, only over his sister because he always gives in to her, like this Christmas, we're looking after their sheep whilst they go on a long holiday."

"Do they do things in return for you?"

Beth has to think about this. Of course Gwenith did come and help out when her parents were ill. Was that doing something for Beth and Gavin or for Gavin and Gwenith's parents? "No, they don't help us," she replies decisively.

"Are you arguing a lot now then, I mean since the referendum?"

"Lots, it's as if we're both ready to jump at anything, whether it's the news, or dealing with the bird flu outbreak or helping out our neighbour this summer when she broke her wrist. All I see is Gavin's negative sides. I can't see, I don't know, I just, I'm not even sure whether I love him, I do love him and I don't, I'm so confused." Beth stares into space.

Samara says gently, "Sex?"

"Sometimes, it's ok."

Samara makes a few more notes. "It's nearly time for us to stop. I think you've been really frank and that's going to be very helpful. How do you yourself feel? Do you think you're going to benefit?"

"I guess so."

"Would you like to make another appointment? I know next

128

week is the week before Christmas and everybody's really busy."

"We've had our busiest weekend. We slaughtered all the geese the weekend just gone and I've made a load of pâté. It's just the two of us this Christmas, plus a load of Gwenith's sheep." Beth adds the last sentence bitterly.

"Ok then, let's make an appointment for next week. In the meantime I want you to do some work for me. Ok?"

"Ok." Beth is glad that Samara doesn't sound patronising.

"Besides the lists, I want you to start speaking to Gavin about the things that bother you. You need to figure out what's important in your marriage and whether these things are worth fighting for. I also want you to write down every time there is a negative thing being said about Brexit and when there is a positive thing being said. I would like you to try and rebalance your reactions so that your emotions aren't going overboard every time you hear the word Brexit being mentioned on the news. How's that?"

"Ok, Sam, I'll try."

"Good, now, how are you fixed for Monday 19 December at 11am?"

Beth checks her phone. "Fine."

"Good, I'll see you then." Samara gives Beth a firm handshake.

Beth leaves the building. She cries all the way to the car. "Let's go and face Gavin," she says to nothing in particular. She feels an enormous sense of trepidation. It's as if something has been staring her in the face for the last year and she hasn't wanted to see it.

Chapter 24 – Confrontational

The telly is on. Beth is watching the comedy without laughing. She has a pen and paper on her lap ready to take notes of pro-Brexit and anti-Brexit jokes. She's been at it now for two days, writing comments at every opportunity, still swearing under her breath at certain comments. Gavin has been observing her in turn and making bemused remarks. "How is this supposed to help you calm down?" That was his comment on the first evening. Beth had answered that there was an alternative; she could start swallowing Valium and become a zombie.

Beth examines her pages at the end of the comedy. She's convinced there's a clear pattern. The news is balanced, equal number of pro and anti-protagonists, the arguments have not gone away and answers are still unclear. Question Time appears to have more pro-Remain audiences. The panellists are equally divided but the audiences are not. Phone-in programmes are dependent upon the channel. Most comedy shows lean towards the piss-take of strong Brexiteers. She concludes that on the whole the more intelligent, the more educated people are arguing against a hard Brexit, whatever that entails. She feels strengthened by it on the one hand but weakened on the other. "The thickos are ruling the asylum," she mutters.

"What was that you said?" Gavin strolls into the living room.

"What was what?"

"What you just said there. I only caught the word asylum."

"Oh, I thought you had left to go to darts."

"I'm off in a minute. I just came in to say goodbye, C'mon, what was it you said?"

"Oh, nothing you need to concern yourself over."

"You've been making notes again I see. Well, is it helping yet?"

Beth still hasn't tackled Gavin properly. She only has the weekend before she's back with Samara and she has plenty to do. She wants to repeat her exact words but knows it will lead to an argument. Part of her wants and needs to clear the air and another part of her is petrified. She takes a deep breath and faces Gavin. "I have noticed something that I think is important. How it helps me I'm not sure as it's partly comforting and partly scary."

"Well, what is it? Talk to me." Gavin sits down on the armchair opposite her. His eyes are demanding; his demeanour is confrontational.

Beth starts quietly. "I have taken notes of all the Brexit discussions. All the time it's discussed on the news or other current affairs programmes, the producers have clearly deliberately made sure they have a balanced panel, two on one side, two on the other side."

Gavin slaps his hand on his knee. "What's the point? The country has voted Brexit so they shouldn't go over all the old arguments again!"

"Ok, I understand why you think so but now the debate is about what kind of Brexit, soft or hard, in the Single Market, out of the Single Market, in the Customs Union, out of the Customs Union…."

Gavin interrupts her. "It's obvious, isn't it? Brexit is Brexit, we leave the lot!"

"You asked me what I've heard and seen, what I said," Beth is beginning to raise her voice. "I'm only telling you what I've noticed!"

"Ok, ok, keep your hair on!"

"So, then there are the phone-in programmes and the comedies. Well, I've listened to Radio 2 and Radio 4 and Radio Wales and also checked some newspapers and seen what people write in response to articles in the main press. The audiences are very different. The more educated people are still by and large arguing for another Referendum."

Gavin jumps up now. "Not another Referendum, Christ no, we couldn't cope with another bleeding Referendum!"

"Will you listen to me or what?" Beth shouts and leaves the sofa. "I can't have a simple single conversation with you about this."

"You don't need to talk to me like this you know!"

"You asked me what it is I said and I wanted to put it in context or I feared you might get cross with me but you get cross with me even when I'm offering you a straightforward analysis."

"Listen to the lecturer making a speech!"

"I give up. I don't want to waste my breath on you. Just go to darts." Beth walks out to the kitchen, puts the kettle on and stares at the dark beyond the window pane. All she sees is a reflection of her own pained face. She is shocked at how old she looks. She hears the backdoor open and close, the car starting and disappearing down the lane.

Beth curls up on the sofa and Googles an old film, something funny from the 1970s, a film that is simply stupid in its contents and not intellectually demanding. She sips her tea. Her brain is screaming out for wine, for obliteration. She recognises all the signs. Laughter is a great distraction.

Two hours later the backdoor opens and Gavin walks in, slightly the worse for wear.

"Hello Cariad, how was your evening taking notes?" Gavin wobbles on his feet as he speaks.

"How did you get home?"

"Our lovely friend Martin dropped me off. Don't worry, I'll fetch the Landrover tomorrow morning. I'll be up early." He slumps on the sofa.

"I'm off to bed. Maybe you should sleep in the spare bedroom. At least you won't keep me awake."

"I don't mind," Gavin slurs, "I'm getting quite used to it, back in my own little bed." He stumbles up the stairs.

Beth waits until he has finished in the bathroom. "Oh well, another night on my own. I'm getting used to it too."

Chapter 25 – Shocked

Beth is up bright and early the next day. She is determined to sort the house and do the Christmas shopping. Gavin has been in the lambing shed for a while so she brings him some coffee. "How are you feeling this morning?"

"I'm ok, thank you." Gavin looks unwashed but apart from that he appears remarkably undamaged by the previous night.

"You haven't been out to fetch your car, surely?"

"No, I don't need it this morning. Martin will pop it over later, and then I'll drive him back."

"How are they doing?"

"Thanks for the coffee. I needed that. They seem to be settling down."

"When is the first batch due?"

"Mid January Owen said. It should be calm until then. Owen has helped to stow the straw bales near the pens so it shouldn't take long to straw them down every day."

"They are lovely sheep. I always did like to see the sheep. Just couldn't cope with the sleepless nights. Have Owen and Gwenith sorted someone to help next month?"

"Well, they had." Gavin sounds uncomfortable. "I had an email this morning to say he can't do it now. He's off to Patagonia on a special work experience trip."

"Great! So who has to sort it?" Beth is annoyed.

"Don't worry Beth, I'll find someone. What are your plans for today?"

"Getting the house ready for Christmas, Christmas shopping, deliver a few cards, that's it really. I could cook dinner if you like."

"That would be lovely. Thanks Cariad. I know you didn't want the sheep here and you won't see much of me over the next few weeks but I want you to know I appreciate it if you can do the dinner."

"You mean cook the dinner every day." Beth's words fall hard on Gavin's ears and they are meant to. He doesn't answer, knows full well that Beth is going to have extra work no matter how lovely a picture he paints. Beth can see right through him. "Well, that's alright then. I'll clean the chicken corner tomorrow and sort out the paperwork from the butcher. Would you like me to phone Llyr to see if one of the Young Farmers can come and help out in January? We can put someone up for a few weeks if it makes life easier." Beth sounds calm and helpful but in her head an angry voice is blaming Gavin for this predicament and past experience tells her that he won't sort it, he'll be too busy, he won't be persuasive enough, and the upshot will be that she is going to end up delivering lambs in the middle of the night, just when she is back at Uni and in need of plenty of sleep.

"You sure you don't mind? I don't want to put you out." Gavin's eyes plead forgiveness.

"I'll get onto it straight after breakfast."

Beth phones Llyr an hour later. He doesn't pick up. She leaves an urgent voicemail, begging him to get back. She washes up, puts the washing away, vacuums the whole house and climbs up the stepladder into the loft to get the Christmas items out, a faded tree, a box with lights and a variety of decorations, some dating back to Gavin's school days. She checks her phone every ten minutes, hoping that Llyr has had her message. She doesn't feel Christmassy. Going through the motions of doing Christmas she had said to Gavin last year. She realises now that even then there had been tensions between the two of them.

She stops for a coffee and opens a box of mince pies to enjoy with it. She has decided not to bake them herself this year. That decision had caused another row with Gavin. She feels like a recalcitrant teenager. How would Sam consider it? Does this fit into a specific list? If so, which one? Beth ponders these questions over her coffee. She actually hasn't put pen to paper yet but she has done a bit of thinking.

She checks her phone again for the umpteenth time. Nothing from Llyr. She looks at the facilities on her phone to write down her lists but she doesn't feel like tapping the words in. It feels too real. She gets the shopping list pad from the kitchen and the pen. The back door opens. She hustles the paper and pen underneath the sofa cushions. Why am I hiding this from Gavin! Beth knows the answer to the question but doesn't want to acknowledge it.

"Oh, I see you're enjoying a mince pie then!"

"I've only just sat down!"

"So? You could have offered me one!"

"I can offer you one now. Do you want coffee?"

"Tea please." Gavin walks out to the bathroom.

Beth retrieves the pen and paper, shoves them in her handbag and puts the kettle on.

"There, tea and a mince pie. Now do you feel Christmas is nearly here?" Beth deliberately looks around the room as if she's an estate agent.

"Oh yes, thanks for putting up the decorations. Are the lights working?"

"Try them!"

Gavin presses the switch. A few dozen coloured lights spring to life. He grins his childish grin at Beth. Christmas is such a big thing to Gavin, she knows, and not to her. Maybe if they'd had children she would have been able to share Gavin's undying enthusiasm, but they haven't and she can't. She can't help but think back to her own childhood experiences and they were so different. It's a gulf between them that can't be bridged. She's sad about it. Beth makes a mental note to write this down for Sam.

"When are you off to the shops?"

"I think I'll leave about two, straight after lunch. I shall drop off a card with Rhian and I really ought to drop Anna's card off too. I'm not sure if I can face it though."

"I can pop it in; I'll do it now before dealing with the cows."

"I've always taken Anna's card. It seems so churlish not to go."

"Then, let's pop over together. We'll say we can't stop because we have Gwenith's sheep, simple!"

"It still feels wrong. It looks like I need a childminder."

"For god's sake, go on your own then Beth!" Gavin marches out of the living room.

"Here we go again, another row, over a bloody card for goodness' sake." Beth looks at the small pile of cards waiting to be delivered. She fishes Anna's out of it. She runs after Gavin. "Ok, let's go together, let's go now."

"Sure?"

"Yes, sure!"

They are home less than ten minutes later. Anna had been grateful that they had both popped in. She hadn't mentioned the previous disastrous visit and subsequent walk-out. She appeared contrite.

"Maybe Mared had a word with her," Beth remarks when they're by the back door.

"Who knows? Anyway, I'm off to the cows. Are you sure you'll be ok to cook dinner?"

"Of course, go on, I'll see you in a bit."

Beth grabs some mince out of the freezer. It is their own. She peels potatoes and cleans some carrots. "One shepherd's pie for a shepherd." She turns the radio on and tunes it to Classic FM, hoping for carols that are not as tacky as the ones on the local commercial station.

As soon as the pie is in the oven, she fetches her handbag, checks her phone again and takes out the piece of paper and pen. "Here goes, nothing from Llyr, might as well get on with my lists."

Beth decides to deal with the positive and negative sides of herself first. She also makes sure she's near her handbag so she can stuff it in when she gets cross and also should Gavin walk in. She feels an uncomfortable but necessary urge for secrecy. She can't be sure the list is the same as the one she wrote last weekend and destroyed. In the background she can hear the Coventry Carol; it's calming.

138

The shepherd's pie is ready when the news comes on. Beth feels too fragile to listen to it. She turns off the radio and puts her list back in her handbag. One list is enough for one day. She calls Gavin and they have a peaceful lunch.

"Have you got a shopping list ready?" Gavin asks her.

The word list brings her up short. It seems bizarre that there are so many words that act like alarm bells in her ears: Brexit, EU migrant, refugee, Trump, sovereignty, control, the list goes on, another list, and now the word list itself.

"Beth, Beth, you ok?" Gavin cuts through her reverie.

"Sorry, I was miles away. You asked if I have a shopping list? No, I haven't." She gets up and tears another piece of paper from the kitchen. The pen is in her handbag. She dashes to the study to fetch another one and hears her phone go off as she returns. She grabs her handbag. "Hopefully it's Llyr!"

Gavin looks up expectantly.

"Hi Llyr, Beth here. Swt i ti?"

Llyr and Beth always speak a mixture of Welsh and English. She explains her reason for calling and begs him to help find a replacement. Llyr promises to do his best. Beth won't relax until a named human being is introduced to her, someone who's capable of being up all night and dealing with triplets and dead lambs.

Gavin gives her an encouraging smile. "Thanks Cariad. I'm sure Llyr will find someone."

"The trouble is that these sheep are lambing when the students are back at Uni so you won't find one of them willing to do it. You can't expect schoolkids to be allowed to do it, however keen they might be."

"Well, as I've said, I'll just have to do the nights. Perhaps we can get a few students to cover during the day!" Gavin is getting het up: he's nervous they won't find someone.

"We can find a foreign worker maybe, if we offer lodgings, like I said earlier."

"What, a New Zealander?"

"I doubt it! Perhaps a Pole."

"I'm not having a bloody Pole living here!"

Beth is so shocked at Gavin's words that at first she just stares at him. Then she says between her teeth with venom in her voice, "What did you just say there? Just you dare to repeat that, will you?"

Gavin looks sheepish. "Well, I won't be able to understand a Pole." It's his best excuse.

"Funny that is because you understand a Belgian perfectly alright." Beth leaves the living room. She takes her handbag upstairs with her, grabs another piece of paper from the kitchen as she passes. "I have something to add to my list," she whispers.

Chapter 26 – Betrayed

Llyr has not found a single person able to help with the sheep. Gavin hasn't done anything to alleviate the situation. Beth has gone through the motions of doing Christmas; she has done the Christmas shopping, she has finished writing the Christmas cards, she has wrapped a few presents, even attended a drinks evening with the Gardening Club and had a meal with her local Liberal Democrat Councillor colleagues. She's barely spoken to Gavin; he's been too busy with the animals and has hardly been in the house. Beth is determined she's going to get the help they need. She Googles and finds some agencies. She emails them and gets some responses. However cross she is with Gavin, she feels she needs to discuss the details with him. That evening over dinner she tackles him.

"I have found cover. I want you to have a look at a few candidates and decide who it is to be, then I'll deal with the booking, get the bedroom ready and sort everything else out."

"Ok, thanks! Where are they from?"

This time Beth loses her cool immediately. She's been holding it in for the whole weekend it seems. She is bursting. "What does it bloody matter where they're from? Whoever comes, can do the job and that's what's important. Will you stop being such a racist piece of shit!"

"How dare you!" Gavin jumps up from his seat. "How dare you call me racist!" he shouts.

Beth shouts back at him. "You shouldn't be concerned about where a person comes from, only if they're capable of doing the job or not. I'm so fed up with…." She doesn't get to finish the sentence.

Gavin is thumping the table and hissing in her face. "The trouble with you is that you don't care enough!"

"I don't care enough! That is the height of hypocrisy coming from you, always telling me that I care too much!" Beth sees red. She snatches the half eaten plates from the table and goes to the kitchen, shouting as she does it. "You don't want this foreign food either then, cooked by a bloody foreigner too!" At the kitchen door she turns round and states coldly. "I tell you what, you sort it out! I shall email you all the details and then you can sort it out yourself!"

The next day Beth is sitting opposite Samara. She hasn't spoken to Gavin since that last row. She can't remember having had an ugly row like that ever before. She feels weepy and angry in equal measure. She has her lists ready to show Samara. She has also done the most sensible thing in writing down the whole row with Gavin. It almost feels too emotional, too painful for her to say it out loud. She has called Gavin a racist, Gavin, the love of her life, husband for 30 years. How did it come to this? Was he always harbouring these thoughts? Has the Brexit vote brought them to the fore? Has he hardened his stance as a result of what he's heard on the news, read in the papers, heard his friends say? Beth's thoughts are gathering all the pieces of information together that have brought her here.

Samara is quietly reading Beth's notes. When she looks up, her eyes show kindness. She acknowledges Beth's suffering and that's enough for Beth to weep uncontrollably.

On the way home Beth stops at a beauty spot. It's a castle ruin. The light is fading but there's enough for Beth to park her car and find a stone wall on which to sit. She needs a quiet half hour to collect her thoughts, to take in what Samara has said, to take in what she herself has said really as Samara mostly listened.

Samara had steered the conversation towards her marriage
142

and had said to Beth that it was ok to be good at lots of things. 'You're not a show-off, you're just a very capable woman. Be proud of it!' Easier said than done when the person closest to her didn't appear to appreciate her. Beth had tried to explain that things between her and Gavin had got a lot worse since the referendum. Samara had not let Beth indulge in bitter rhetoric about Brexit. Beth is trying to recall the exact words Samara used. They were along the line of 'The vote has been taken and you need to adjust yourself to this new situation'.

Beth looks around her. The oncoming darkness appears to seep into her body, into her soul, her heart, her brain. There's nobody around, no other car to be seen, just distant headlights. Suddenly Beth is scared. The fear is of all the unknowns, the unseens, the unpredictables. She also feels terrified that her marriage is at an end. And then she's angry, angrier than she's ever been before. She screams out loud. The sound doesn't travel far. It emboldens her. "Fuck Gavin, fuck all you Brexiteers, fuck Anna, fuck Rhian, fuck Samara too! I'll be fucked if I'm going to fucking adjust to any of you, fucking ever again, you can all fuck off, the fucking lot of you!"

Beth's voice is echoing off the castle wall. She hammers her fists on it and shouts until she's exhausted herself.

At home there's a letter waiting for her. It's from the Home Office. She pours a glass of wine, leaves the letter untouched. She doesn't want Gavin to see her lose her temper so checks his whereabouts. He's busy in the lambing shed. Beth walks over to him but says nothing. Gavin looks terrible. He clearly hasn't had much sleep despite his hard days.

"Hello Beth, how was your day?" Beth stays silent. She knows Gavin is waiting for an apology from her. She will apologise if she's sure she's wrong. For now they are living like strangers. Gavin is the one who is cracking first. Beth thinks harshly,

'Yeh, he needs me more than I need him!'

"A letter came for you, from the Home Office. Maybe it's good news, eh?" Gavin tries a second time.

Beth shrugs her shoulders.

"Sorry, I haven't done anything about dinner yet. Oh for God's sake Beth, you're not going to keep this up over Christmas, are you?"

Beth says coldly: "I'll get something out of the freezer. How long are you going to be?"

"Forty minutes at most. Please Beth!" Gavin pleads but Beth has already turned round and is walking out of the shed. "Shit, fucking shit!" she hears him as she reaches the door. Gavin is totally frustrated.

Beth rummages through the freezer until she finds something she can shove in the microwave. She looks for Gavin's laptop and opens it. He has never used a password. She has never had cause to check his stuff out; has only ever helped him learn how to deal with something new to him. This time she immediately goes to his email inbox. She wants to make sure he has read the details of the agencies. It's as if she wants more ammunition to fire at him.

The email box is fairly full; Gavin hasn't had time to deal with things. She quickly scans for her own email. He has read it. She checks the sent mails to find out if he's dealt with the 'problem'. Nothing for the last week. She goes back to the inbox and starts to take note of where the rest of the emails have come from. She weirdly feels like a spy. There are loads from Facebook. Gavin has never shown any interest in Facebook! She has never had a friend request from him!

The world starts spinning round in Beth's head. Through the mire she hears the backdoor opening. Automatically, she
144

closes the server, shuts down the laptop and walks into the kitchen.

"So, are you going to tell me what was in that letter?" Gavin sounds as if he is keeping a lid on his emotions.

Beth remains mute. She thinks, 'Are you going to tell me your secrets or am I going to have to find out for myself?' She puts the plates of food in front of them and eats like a zombie.

"Right, I can't stand this atmosphere any longer!" Gavin is beginning to lose his cool. "What do I need to do to get you to talk to me?"

"Sort out help with the sheep." Beth's face is blank, her voice level.

"I'm dealing with it! It will be sorted!"

Beth looks at him sceptically.

"I am! You've sent me the details and I've emailed a few of these people."

Now Beth knows he's lying. She doesn't let on; she wants to know the full extent of his deceit. She bends her head to the table in order to hide her face. Stay hard, stay calm, stay strong, she tells herself.

Gavin disappears back to the shed straight after dinner. Beth feels her shoulders relax. She picks up her glass of wine; she hadn't touched it. Time to read the letter.

It's precisely what Beth expected. It states nothing new, in fact it states nothing. There is no reassurance for people from the EU, no reassurance for Beth in her personal situation, just more addresses she can write to, the Department of Work and Pensions for a pension forecast, the Department of Health for sanctioning her use of the NHS or maybe proscription. The letter is bland, the language bureaucratic, non-committal. She leaves it on the table for Gavin to find.

She looks at Gavin's laptop as if it's poison. She wants to investigate further but doesn't want to touch it. It feels contaminated. His fingers have been on it. Has he tapped horrible messages on Facebook? She feels paranoid. How can she be so distrustful of Gavin?

Gavin enters the living room. He sees Beth staring in front of her. "Beth."

Beth looks at him. Her face is full of pain.

"Beth, we have a problem."

"Too right we have a problem!" It comes out more sarcastic than Beth had intended.

"I know you and I have a problem but we have an immediate problem right now with the sheep!" Gavin sounds impatient.

"Oh! What?"

"A few of them are obviously in labour. I knew some of them were due in early Jan but this is two weeks early. Can you please come and have a look?"

"I'll be right there. Are the gloves in the shed?"

"It's all ready."

Beth switches into professional mode where she herself has no part. She nips to the toilet, scrubs her hands and slips on her overall. Within minutes she is checking out the sheep Gavin is worried about. "They're in labour alright. Can we separate them from the rest of the flock?"

"I'll put the hurdles up. You keep an eye on them. Then we'll

146

get them into their own pens."

"I think we still have some colostrum in the freezer. I spotted it when I was looking for supper."

"You think we'll need it?"

"Depends on how many lambs these ewes have."

Gavin finishes the hurdles and between them they calmly get the ewes in the individual pens. "Thanks Cariad, thanks for helping me."

"I wouldn't Cariad me too soon. I'm doing this for the poor sheep."

Gavin just wants to hear Beth talk again so he carries on. "Do you think it's toxoplasmosis?"

"Don't know. Could be twin lamb disease. We'll probably have to call the vet tomorrow." She sounds business-like.

"Yes, of course. I'll be ok for a bit now. Do you want to go and find that colostrum? Perhaps you can bring me a flask of coffee, if you don't mind?"

Beth looks at Gavin's worried face. She doesn't want to lose any lambs any more than Gavin does. She is still really cross with him. But a crisis is a crisis. "Tell you what, I'll bring you a flask and go to bed. I'll take over from you at two."

"Beth, are you sure?" Gavin is so happy.

"You make sure you find extra help tomorrow!" Beth's tone is sharp.

When Beth is back in the house, she glances at Gavin's laptop. There's no time for trawling through his Facebook pages now; it'll have to wait till the crisis is over.

Chapter 27 – Caring

The alarm at 2am shakes Beth out of a deep sleep. She feels physically sick at being woken so rudely but strangely ready to climb out of bed. Her old clothes are lying ready for her; she'd made sure of that when she got upstairs the evening before. Downstairs she makes herself a large flask of coffee, takes a tin and fills it with some delicious Christmas snacks, grabs the radio and torch and heads out into the dark and cold.

Gavin is pleased to see her. He briefly updates her on the situation and gratefully retires.

Beth rewires her brain. Gavin will be back at 8am to relieve her. This is how they used to do it when they had their own sheep. She has a strange sense of deja vu. The comfy chair is in the same old position. The old duvet is on top of it to keep her warm. The fridge is working. It has plenty of little bottles of colostrum in it. She had sorted them out last night too. The old kettle and old pan are ready too for warming the bottles. She notices that Gavin has left several bottles which are still partially full.

She checks the weeny lambs that have been born in the night. "Oh, you little cutie, let's have a look at you." Beth picks up a tiny lamb. The mother isn't bothered. She's licking another titchy one. "That's it, you give her a good clean. And how are you doing, mum?" Beth is acutely aware that she naturally talks to the animals as if they understand every word she says, that her voice is that of a mother with young children. She thinks she probably would have made a very good mother. Don't get depressed over that, she tells herself sternly, you have enough to get worked-up over.

She warms a couple of bottles and expertly gets each lamb to drink. Both bottles are emptied and the lambs lay down to sleep with their mother. "See you both at four. Stay alive."

Beth goes to the next pen. One of the lambs has succumbed. She removes the little body into the corner of the shed. It looks pathetic. Beth makes sure its sister drinks a whole bottle and checks the ewe.

She spots the ewe in the next pen is about to give birth. "I'm on my way, I'm on my way." Ten minutes later two more titchy lambs are struggling for life. Beth's patience pays off. The mother suckles them while Beth holds them up. "That's it, now let's move you little ones into a cosy corner so your poor mum can get rid of her afterbirth."

Beth is amazed that an hour has gone by when she manages to sit down and pour herself a coffee. Her hands are grubby and she removes the worst on a wet-wipe. She tucks into some biscuits and looks around contentedly. What peace!

The next three hours are spent feeding lambs, clearing away a few afterbirths, removing another dead lamb, drinking coffee and munching on snacks. By six Beth is exhausted. She needs to stay awake for another couple of hours. She remembers how she always hated the last two hours. Time for turning on the radio. She fiddles with the tuning knob. They never used to lamb this early in the year she perceives, or late to be precise, as station after station blares out Christmas ditties. She doesn't want to listen to Radio 4 as she can't cope with hearing politicians blabbing about Brexit, not now. She finds a station that is playing non-stop music from the good old days, the sixties and seventies, with intermittent carols. It'll have to do.

The music is soothing, yet not so relaxing that Beth will fall asleep to it. She makes another round of the shed. In the corner her chickens are beginning to stir. It's still pitch dark outside but the shed's lights are affecting them. Beth throws them some seeds. "We might as well all be awake."

She feeds the surviving lambs the last of the bottles of

colostrum. She tries to get all the ewes to suckle their little offspring. Two of them manage well. "I won't be able to go to bed at eight, will I? I'll have to go to the farm shop and get some more colostrum! I can't have you lot dying on me, no!" Beth's voice is sweet and placid. The sheep relax with her near them.

By seven the coffee has all gone, as have the snacks. The shed is in sleeping mode. Even the chickens have decided to have a lie-in after all. Beth stretches her legs under the duvet. She concentrates on the radio in order to stop herself dropping off. She hums along to the tune. She recognises it vaguely. She doesn't know the words but becomes aware of them. It's as if the singer is singing words that she herself has been saying for the last few months. 'I am I said, I am said I, and I am lost and I don't even know why, leaving me lonely still.'

Beth is completely awake now. Who is that singing? She listens attentively to the announcer. "That was Neil Diamond with 'I am I said'."

"Neil Diamond! Never heard of him, must be before my time. I'll Google him." Beth feels excited but at the same time she keeps hearing the words in her ears and senses the total sadness in his voice.

A Christmas hit from the seventies breaks her reverie. She turns the radio off, gets up to wander around the shed again. She sings the words quietly under her breath, the same ones over and over again. She's still singing when Gavin comes in to relieve her.

"You're singing, you must've had a good night." Gavin is looking more human. He has clearly slept well and he's had a shower.

"Well, it's my way of staying awake. I can't go to bed just yet, I'll have to get more colostrum. Some of them are suckling

150

nicely but not all. Two dead lambs I'm afraid. I've left them in the corner over there with the afterbirths. I haven't noticed any more in labour. Hopefully, the rest will come when they're due. I'll take these empty bottles, have some breakfast and a shower, then I'll be off to the farm shop."

"I need to see to the cows at some point. When do you want to catch up on your sleep?"

"As soon as I get back but I can wait till you've dealt with the cows. I'll get the bottles ready and then leave you to it till midday if that's ok?"

"That's brilliant." Gavin walks over to Beth who is by the shed door with her arms full. He leans over to kiss her but she turns away from him.

"Sorry Gavin, I'm really not in the mood. I can't just pretend we're ok. See you later." Beth walks out, leaving Gavin defeated.

Chapter 28 – Secret

The next two days go by in a fug of half-awakeness, deep sleep, feeding lambs, cooking, cleaning and trying to fit in dealing with the demands of chickens and cows. Beth and Gavin pass each other at 2am, 8am, midday, dinner and 8pm. It's a weird routine. Every time they meet, Beth asks Gavin if he's sorted help for January and every time he reassures her that he has.

The lambs have stopped coming. The vet agreed with Beth that it was twin lamb disease caused by stress of moving and that the rest should be fine. They hope they can both sleep again at night and only get up to do the night feeding.

On the third day Beth gets up at ten in the morning. She wants to get her sleep rhythm back to normal. Gavin is not expecting her to relieve him till midday. He's promised to leave her to sleep in peace.

She looks at his laptop. There is a strange feeling in her gut. Yet, she has to do this. She opens it and shuts it straightaway. She opens her own laptop instead, stares at the screen as it slowly fills with familiar symbols. She clicks on her emails. There are only a few to deal with, a few Christmas cards, the rest are holiday offers and petitions. Next she checks her Facebook page. It's full of other people's happy Christmas recipes and parties and more petitions, many the same ones as she's had in her inbox. She dutifully signs them all. She is particularly pleased to see the old Remain campaigners and some new groups calling for fair treatment of European Migrants. She leaves a few comments, shares them on her Lib Dem local Facebook page and wishes them well.

She feels her own negativity pressing in her chest. Only a few months ago she was arguing on the streets, she wrote to newspapers, made her speech at the Refugees Need Our Help meeting, was happy with her profile in the Herald, and now?

Now she feels as if the emptiness inside her is never going to be filled. She can stand on the street corner with hundreds of other people, all feeling angry at being called 'Bargaining Chips', all worried over their future, all keen for this limbo in their lives to be over, so they can get back to normal, but for Beth there's something else missing so that normal is not pre-referendum normal.

It's eleven. She still has one hour. She simply has to bite the bullet. She opens Gavin's laptop and this time forces herself to leave it to boot up. Gavin's familiar icons pop up. She opens his email inbox. She doesn't detect anything from the agencies. She opens his sent folder. Nothing new. Gavin has lied to her several times a day over the last few days. Beth is more upset than angry. She goes back to the inbox and scrolls down to the last Facebook message Gavin has opened. Somebody sent him a 'like'. Once on the Facebook page she presses home. Her heart is beating in her throat. This is Gavin's homepage. He has a pseudonym. She was expecting that. 'MeatloafBachgen'! It's kind of funny but so childish! She checks his settings, his friends, reads a load of posts and looks at the photographs. She was not expecting this.

She leaves everything as she found it, closes the laptop and heads for the shower. Under the hot water she scrubs herself. She can't scrub out the thoughts. Gavin's behaviour over the last year is thoroughly clear to her now. She knows what he'll say. He hadn't wanted to hurt her and he knew how deeply she felt about it all, blah, blah, blah.

It's midday. Gavin is expecting her in the lambing shed. She doesn't want to confront him. Not yet. Beth gets in the car and drives off. She spots Gavin at the shed door shouting something after her. Seconds later her phone rings. She ignores it. She turns towards town. She has another three hours of daylight. It should be heaving in town two days before Christmas. She passes the shopping centre and heads for the University. Her phone has rung at least four times when she pulls into the deserted car-park.

Once in the office she realises she has had nothing to eat yet. Her stomach is rumbling. She takes her purse and her Uni keys and heads for the lovely cafe she's been to with Naomi. She fills her belly with hot spicy soup and a home-made bread roll. She orders a huge chunk of cake and has a herbal tea with it. She breathes in the consoling smells of the cafe, fills her lungs as if the odours will be able to protect her from her up and coming struggles.

Beth makes for the bank, asks to make a large transfer from their joint bank account into her savings account. She also stops a variety of Direct Debits and asks that her salary is paid into her savings account directly. The lady behind the counter frowns at Beth. "I'm making my New Year's resolution early," Beth grimaces, "I'm going to try and put more money away for my old age."

"Good idea," laughs the bank clerk.

"And all the unnecessaries have to go!" adds Beth.

She heads back to the Uni. The temptation to check her phone is too great. Gavin has phoned and texted about every ten minutes. Rhian has tried to contact her too, no doubt on Gavin's request. She deletes the lot.

She makes herself a coffee and sits in the window. The view is as she expects it, yet she looks at it with different eyes today. She scans the sky for seabirds and starlings. She examines rooftop lines and chimney stacks. She stares out to sea, knowing it's far too far to see the splash of a dolphin but wishing to spot something exciting all the same. The sunset will be early. The grey overhead clouds don't promise a beauty.

At 4pm she is heading back to the farm. She has done what

she came to do. She now needs to be resolved to carry out the next stage.

Several times on the way back she stops the car. At one point she gets out and gulps lungfuls of sea air. She is nervous, she's upset but also strangely dry-eyed. She thinks she's cried so much these last few months that her tear ducts have packed in.

At 5pm she pulls into the farm track. She sits in the car and wishes to stay until she has the courage to get out. It's not to be. Gavin has been looking and listening for her and comes rushing out the door.

"Where the hell have you been?" Gavin sounds both angry and relieved in the same breath.

"I had to sort a few things out in town." Beth manages to just stay calm enough to keep her voice level while she pulls a box from the car. She brushes past Gavin and heads for the back door.

"You could have told me! You were going to relieve me at twelve! You could have answered your phone, but nothing, you told me nothing!" Gavin is ranting at Beth's cold face.

Taste of your own medicine she says out loud in her head, you don't like it, do you?

"Well!" Gavin is standing with his hands on his hips waiting for Beth to say something. She simply takes the box upstairs and ignores him. He is still shouting at her from the bottom of the stairs. She has to get away from him, find some more strength. She decides to go to the lambing shed, have some snacks, put her thoughts in order and deal with Gavin in the evening.

"I'm off to the shed, you have some rest." Her outer portrayal is a state of total levelness.

"What about supper!" Gavin is clearly confused by her behaviour.

"I'm not bothered myself. Sort yourself something." Beth grabs a flask and her box of goodies. She starts to put on her wellies.

"Beth, for god's sake, what's the bloody matter?" This time Gavin is almost quiet. His eyes are full of questions.

"Later," she simply states, "I'll talk to you later."

Chapter 29 – Decisive

The shed is cold but under the old duvet it is snug and secure. The lambs are thriving and the chickens have gone to bed. Beth takes out a small wallet from her pocket, her new phone. She has spent an hour on her Uni computer downloading music. She has finished with heavy metal; Neil Diamond is her new favourite. She plugs in her earphones and puts him on repeat. 'I am I said'! The words soak into her until she feels saturated with his voice.

At seven Gavin appears in front of her. He notices the tin of goodies is empty and the flask unscrewed. Beth is calmly eyeing him from behind the plastic cup. Her face is inscrutable. She reaches into her pocket and fiddles with the phone for the off button. Neil Diamond was just singing, 'Leaving me lonely still'.

"Surely you've finished here!" Gavin's voice is gruff.

"Yes, I have. I was enjoying the peace and quiet," Beth replies. "Why don't you go in and I'll follow in a few minutes."

Gavin goes off like a poodle. Beth pulls the earphones out, checks her phone is off, gathers her things and turns the lights off. She stands outside the backdoor. An owl is hooting not far away. Lights are flashing across the road. She hates these garish Christmas accessories. "Oh well, let's get this over and done with." Her own voice, even whispered, sounds like an intrusion into the December night.

"You want a glass of wine?"

"No thanks. I bought some herbal tea today and I've just had a whole flask full."

"Herbal tea!" Gavin almost spits the words out.

"Yes, never mind that. It's my choice. You have wine or beer or whatever!" Beth sounds more abrupt than she wants to; she's desperate to stay calm.

Gavin pours himself a glass of wine. "So, why couldn't you be bothered to tell me where you were going today?"

"I'll answer that when you tell me why you haven't bothered to find cover."

"I have!" he shouts defensively.

"And why you keep lying to me."

"I'm not!"

"Show me the response you've had."

Gavin looks bewildered but only briefly. "What's this all about? Come on Beth?"

"Show me the response you've had from the agencies I forwarded to you."

"You're not my mother you know!"

"I'm your wife and I deserve to know the truth. You've been lying to me, stop trying to dig a hole. You haven't found cover because you haven't contacted the agencies."

"I bloody well have! Stop being Mrs High and Mighty!"

"Show me the response!" Beth is getting a bit impatient.

"I'll have cover in place; I told you I would and I will, you don't…."

Beth interrupts him. "You have not done it. I know you

158

haven't and I know you've been lying to me. I checked your inbox and your sent box and you haven't even bothered to ask the agencies for cover." She watches his eyes. They are angry but she feels angrier. Her anger is keeping her from shouting. His anger is childish, as childish as his Facebook page name she figures.

"How could you?" They are the only words Gavin manages to utter. "How could you go and check my private emails!"

"If you want to keep things private, you should put a password on your laptop!"

"I will, I!" Gavin looks as if his pride has been wounded but Beth ignores his pronouncements.

"No need any more because I won't be looking at your emails ever again."

"What d'you mean?" Gavin is waking up to Beth's matter of fact tone of voice. He looks alarmed.

"I won't be looking at your laptop or at anything else on this farm again. I won't be looking at you again. I'm leaving you. I'm packing my stuff tonight." There, it's out now, she thinks, and the relief is overwhelming. She had thought she might burst into tears but she actually feels like smiling, like laughing out loud.

"Beth, you are joking, you are."

"I'm being totally serious."

"All because I haven't had time to find cover and I told you I had 'cos I didn't want to worry you or I wanted you to stop going on about it."

Beth waits patiently for him to finish his sentence. She looks at him intently, making sure he is taking note of what she is about to say.

"All because you are a liar. You are a liar and a deceiver. How long do you think I have been unhappy? How long has it taken you to notice that I wasn't coping? Your behaviour has fooled me and confused me. But it's all totally clear to me now. I don't want to live with MeatloafBachgen."

Gavin puts his head in his hands. He sits there for a few minutes. Beth can see his shoulders go up and down. She waits for the excuses, the tears, the pleading with her. She watches his head lift. His eyes are beautiful.

"Please Beth, I shouldn't have written some of those things but I felt so frustrated."

"No, you shouldn't have written the things you have. We are all entitled to our opinion and mine has been clear from the start of this bloody awful referendum campaign." Beth can no longer keep her emotions under control.

"Yes, I know, but I didn't agree with you!"

"You didn't agree with me but you never said so! You just didn't come out and support me and the reason for that is because you're a bloody racist!" Beth jumps up and her eyes are aflame. "You may have supported Brexit like so many other idiotic Welsh farmers but you are married to me! To a Belgian! And as your wife I could have expected support from you but you were too busy with your UKIP mates writing awful stuff on Facebook about bloody foreigners! How do you think that makes me feel? Well?" Beth is shouting this demand at Gavin who is looking wretched.

"I got sucked into it." His excuse is as feeble as his voice.

"Oh, poor little Gavin, poor MeatloafBachgen, can't think for

160

himself!"

"It wasn't like that."

"It wasn't, was it? And what do you think it's been like for me this last half year? And what do you think it's been like for Sophia and for her Romanian friends?"

Gavin reaches for his glass of wine and takes a large gulp. Beth can't resist a retort. "Who's reaching for the bottle now then!"

"Please stop Beth, please can we sit down and have a civilised conversation. I promise I'll make it all up to you." Gavin looks at her with his wet eyes pleading.

She takes a deep breath. "Ok, I'll calm down. But there really is nothing left for me to say." She feels her resolve strengthening as his eyes remain on hers. She sees a pathetic boy who has been borne away on a tide of ill-informed Euro bashing racist comments, most of them from his so-called friends. She sees the pathetic boy who has been relying on her for 30 years and who has not been there for her to lean on in her hour of greatest need. She sees a boy who needs to learn to stand on his own two feet. She sees a boy.

"I'm going upstairs to pack. I shall be gone this evening. I wish you well with the farm. I'll miss the farm." She wishes she hadn't said those last few words as she feels tears pricking. "You can have all the farm. I don't want anything. I just want to take my personal stuff." She gets up and walks out the living room door. She can hear Gavin crying loudly, sobbing.

Upstairs she puts the earplugs in. Neil Diamond's words are filling her brain once more. 'Leaving me lonely still'. Lonely, she thinks, yes I've been so lonely, so bloody lonely. And now Gavin will be lonely. How did it come to this?

Chapter 30 – Reminiscing

Once in the bedroom she takes a good look round. The bed, the enormous bed, she's had it to herself for many nights the last few months. Do I have to strip it, she thinks? The large built-in wardrobe, her clothes neatly folded, her dresses hanging. She opens it, shuts it again, sits on the edge of the bed and weeps. She still has tears left; her tear ducts have not packed up. She blows her nose. The empty box she picked up in town today is staring at her, making her feel both guilty and desperate. She pulls her old phone out of her handbag and checks it. Nothing important. She tips the rest of the handbag's contents on the bed. Among the pieces of paper and make-up she spots the lists. Samara had given them back to her, 'to refer to in times of crisis'. Those were her exact words. Beth reads them twice. She realises she's leaving Gavin for good reasons but the actual doing it is hard, bloody hard.

The door opens. Gavin is standing on the threshold. He too is looking around the room and visibly going through his memories. This had been his parents' room. After their deaths he and Beth designed it together to create a haven of bliss. They had chosen the bed and the bedding with lovemaking on their minds. He had built the en-suite bathroom himself and the walk-in wardrobes. She had painted the room in the tastiest manner. She had added some beautiful paintings she'd bought at a local auction.

"You haven't packed anything." Gavin breaks the awkward silence.

"No, I'm deciding what to take. I can't fit much in my little car. I've already loaded the boot with stuff from my office." Beth pulls the earphones out and shoves them with the new phone in her handbag.

"Why?" Gavin is genuinely surprised.

162

"I shan't be staying at the Uni."

"Where will you go?"

"Sorry, but I don't think it matters to you."

"It does actually; you matter to me."

"I don't want to go over everything again. Please, just let me pack."

"But we must sort things out. You can't just walk out and leave me in the lurch!" Gavin is getting angry again.

"Really Gavin, you'll have your farm and I'll live my life somewhere else. Whatever I leave behind you can dump or take to the charity shop."

"That's not what I'm on about! What am I going to do with the animals, on my own?"

"Why don't you think about it? You'll manage." She wants to add that he can always contact the agencies but lets it go, the arguments are over.

She gets off the bed. Somehow the job seems easier in his presence. He annoys her to such an extent that she feels she can be quick and decisive. She pulls a lovely dress out of the wardrobe. Gavin had helped her choose it for a major planning conference. It will always remind her of Gavin. She throws it on the bed. "That should fetch at least £10 in the Cancer Research shop!"

Gavin watches her from the door in total disbelief as she sorts all her clothes into piles. It takes her less than five minutes. The one and only suitcase they possess is only half full when she's done. She adds the book to it from the bedside cupboard that she's halfway through reading.

"Excuse me, can I pass, I need to go to the spare bedroom and check for stuff there." Gavin moves only partly so she has to brush past him to get out.

The spare bedroom is in a mess. Gavin hasn't bothered to change the bedding or remove his dirty washing from the floor. The window has clearly been left shut for weeks; it reeks like a teenage boy's bedroom. Beth quickly grabs the few ornaments she knows are hers as well as her walking boots. She can't stand the stench.

Gavin is sitting on the edge of the bed reading her notes when she re-enters. He looks up. "Quite a list of things that bug you about me!"

Beth grabs the pieces of paper. "Do you mind, those are my private things."

"Oh, and you care about privacy, the woman who goes sneaking through my private emails!" Gavin is suitably sarcastic.

"Well, if you really want to know, these are lists that Sam asked me to draw up! Not that it matters anyway, not anymore. You can burn those. I shan't be seeing Sam anymore either." Beth shoves the few ornaments amongst her clothes as she speaks.

"Who's Sam? Another one of your little student friends?"

"Sam, Samara, is the counsellor you were so keen for me to visit. Draw up some lists she said. Write down all the things that bug you. Well, they're all in front of you."

"Yes, and they're all me! Everything's my fault while you're so damn perfect!"

"Funny you say that, as I actually completely ran myself down

164

when I saw Sam. But you're right about the things that bug me; it's to do with you! And that's why I'm off!"

"I thought it was Brexit!"

"Yes, of course it's Brexit that bugs me. Has it ever occurred to you that I might have been able to cope with Brexit had you been on the Remain side and supported me?" Beth is yelling back at Gavin whilst struggling to do a zip up on the side of the suitcase.

"Wherever you go in this country, you'll be dealing with Brexit!"

"Yeh, but not with a husband on the other side! Now, if you don't mind, I need to get on as I still have all the downstairs to go through." Beth snatches up a few items in the bathroom and on the dressing table, lifts the suitcase and reaches for her handbag and the bits lying loose on the bed.

Gavin takes her wrist. Beth tries to pull back instinctively. Gavin is strong and holds her firmly. "Please Beth, can I at least explain to you why I voted Brexit and why I felt I couldn't talk to you about it?" He is looking into her fuming eyes.

"Let go of me! Let me go downstairs!" Her voice is almost menacing.

"Promise me you'll sit down and hear me out."

"Are you blackmailing me?"

"I just want you to understand; I just want to set the record straight. You may still want to stay. Please Beth!" Gavin sounds desperate.

"You can talk to me as I pack. I'll not change my mind but you can do your best to justify your comments and your behaviour. I promise I'll listen. I warn you though; I might actually really start hating you, while for now I'm just full of contempt."

Gavin stares at Beth. She is looking taller and more confident than she has in a while. He drops her wrist.

Beth reaches the bottom of the stairs in a flash. Gavin follows slowly with the empty box in his hand. "You left this."

"Oh, thanks!" Beth takes the box and her handbag and goes to the study, the most difficult room of all. She has collected an enormous amount of books over the years and there's no way she has time to go through them now nor the space in the car to take them. She automatically picks up some well-used favourites and puts them in the bottom of the box. She has to simply leave the rest. Thoughts of her aunt Celia leaving everything behind on her deathbed remind her that life is transitory. Her 30 years with Gavin may have been 60% of her life so far but it's still transitory.

Gavin stands in the doorway again, a spectator. He can observe what Beth packs but can't see her face. Had he been able to, he would have found it unreadable. "So, I've been a farmer all my life, an independent farmer."

Beth thinks she could react but decides to leave him to ramble. He'll notice soon enough how dependent he's been on her. Not that she particularly relishes him suffering but she does want him to face reality. She opens the drawers and takes out all her certificates and other important papers. The drawer with the bills and bank stuff in she leaves closed. "Carry on, I'm listening." She keeps her back towards Gavin as she carefully makes sure everything fits in the box.

"Well, I can't stand the interference from Brussels, sorry, I mean the EU bureaucrats."

"Ok." Beth's flat voice gives nothing away. She carries the box to the backdoor and goes to the living room, followed by Gavin. He leans on the edge of the table.

"I just feel fed up with all the rules and regulations and want us in Wales to make our own. We're a proud nation and can deal with the world on our own terms."

Beth is carefully wrapping up Celia's ornaments. She tucks them amongst her clothes in the suitcase. Carry on talking crap Gavin, she thinks. She even has to repress a smile.

"I discussed it with my farming mates and we all agreed we'd be better off outside the EU, we can create our own opportunities."

Beth moves to the dining room. A few ornaments remain to be packed. The last major thing to be tackled is the sideboard, a beautiful old Welsh dresser that had belonged to Gavin's grandparents. She doesn't want the jugs; she removed them to the inside of the dresser after the last funeral. The two drawers though have their collection of photographs in them, their holiday snaps, pre-digital age, family photos, and their wedding day photographs. She feels a momentary pang. She faces Gavin. He is looking like a sad schoolboy and is standing at the door again.

"Can I just say that all you've been saying there I've heard from Brexit campaigners. Nothing you've said explains why you made anti-immigrant comments on Facebook, nothing you've said explains why you are friends on Facebook with the very people who have abused me, nothing you've said explains why you like their racist comments, nothing you've said explains why you carried on even though you knew that these comments were bloody painful to me, nothing you've said explains why you hid all that behaviour behind the so-called caring husband who sorted out the abuse, nothing you've said explains why you couldn't be bothered to get help with the lambing, but it is all explained in a very simple way, you just can't stand foreigners and that, in my opinion, includes me!" Throughout this speech Beth has become more and more passionate while Gavin is hanging his head. He really has nothing to say in answer. "Now, if you say you love me and you want me to have a small grain of respect left for you, I want you to promise me something."

"What?" Gavin asks meekly.

"That you'll sort the photographs out. I don't want any with you in it, just the ones with me alone. Can you scan them in please and email them to me?"

"Of course."

Beth wheels the now stuffed suitcase to the hall and puts it next to the box. She goes to the kitchen. She gets a carrier bag and fills it to the brim with goodies. She adds a bottle of wine and an opener. She makes a final flask of her new special tea. She loads the car. Gavin offers to help but she shrugs him off. "The animals need your help, I don't."

She grabs her coat and scarves and hats, her shoes and wellies. She dumps them on the spare seat next to her. She locks the passenger door and opens the driver's one. "Goodbye Gavin. I wish you a good future. I hope you think happy thoughts about your last 30 years."

"Beth, please, I've been wrong, I don't want you to go, I love you!" Gavin is struggling to speak through his tears.

Beth is glad she spent some time with the sheep and the chickens earlier; she sort of said goodbye. Now she wants to go and say a final goodbye to them. She wishes to go for a walk through the fields and say goodbye to the cows in the dark barn. She wishes to hear the owl hoot. She looks at Gavin and turns. Best just to go.

168

Chapter 31 – Vengeful

"I'd like a room for tonight please. I'm sorry I'm this late. I hope it isn't a problem."

The receptionist smiles a courteous smile at Beth and hands her a form. "No problem, welcome to the Glan-y-Môr. Can you just fill the details please?"

Beth writes a false name, false address, Gavin's mobile number, Gavin's truck number plate and leaves the email space blank. "There you are. You won't need my email address. I'm passing through. I also won't need breakfast tomorrow morning as I'm leaving quite early."

"We can do breakfast at seven am if you like."

"I'll be gone by then, but thanks."

"Can I have your card details?"

"I would rather pay cash." Beth is beginning to feel like a criminal. She wants to get away from reception as soon as possible. She doesn't want Peter Mezzo to spot her. The receptionist is clearly not Welsh. Beth can't identify the accent. Neither is the receptionist bothered. She hands Beth the key to her bedroom.

"Take the lift here. Your room is on the second floor. Turn right when you get out of the lift. I hope you have a pleasant night." The tone is flat, not unpleasant but neither welcoming.

"Thanks." Beth takes the key and her handbag.

"Do you need a hand with your luggage?" Beth swears the receptionist is almost sneering.

"I'll manage, thank you," Beth grimaces back.

Once in the room she locks the door and sighs a huge sigh of relief. This is the last place Gavin will expect her to be. Not that he has time to come searching for her, nor that she thinks he's inclined to do so, but she wishes to be out of his reach all the same. And she has an ulterior motive.

Beth empties her handbag on the bed. She has added some clean underwear, her toothbrush and toothpaste. Her new phone beckons. She also tips an indelible pen out of the bag, another item bought in town in the afternoon and stowed in the glove compartment.

There are tea and coffee making facilities in the room. The décor is in the latest minimalist style. Beth loathes it. The bathroom is splendid though. Beth runs a deep bubble bath. She switches on the telly. She makes a hot chocolate, strips and relaxes in the soap suds.

The events of the last few days tumble dreamlike through her brain. She could have said so much more to Gavin. He never gave her any satisfactory answers. Did she give him a fair chance? She figures he had ample opportunity over the last six months to be straight with her and he lied, he deceived her over and over again. It's the thing she copes with the least. How could he sit on the sofa pretending he was feeling sorry for her receiving all those hateful emails, messages, tweets, when all along he knew his mates were sending some of them and he agreed with their point of view? Oh, he may not have wanted her to hang herself or get raped or go back to where she came from but he still wanted a stop to foreigners, to people like her! Had Gavin been really such a split person, such a Jekyll and Hyde? Was it possible that he loved her, even though she is a foreigner, yet be opposed to foreigners coming to Wales, opposed to foreigners in ways that were inexplicable to her! Did he just not see her as a foreigner? She sips her hot chocolate and recalls a conversation she had way back before the referendum. Didn't he say then, 'I don't see you as a foreigner'. Out loud she says, "You didn't see me at all." Her voice echoing off the clean walls stirs her into action.

She dries herself thoroughly, then drapes a second large towel around her as a dressing gown. She hangs her clothes over a chair ready for her early start. She puts the alarm for five on her old phone and turns it off.

"Now then, where shall I start?"

Beth picks up the pen. "Dressing table first I think."

The pen is a deep red, blood red. In large bold letters she writes,

REMAINERS PISS ON YOUR BRITISH COCKS!

She looks at her handiwork. How satisfying this is. She finally understands how angry young people feel who have a crazy urge to plaster every conceivable surface with graffiti.

The tall mirror on the wall is her next target. She carefully fits in the words,

PM AND YOUR RACIST MATES,

ENJOY THE MESS,

I MEAN THE BREXIT MESS!

The telly is getting too loud for Beth. She turns it off; she wasn't listening to it in any case, just using it as wallpaper. She can hear tellies on in other bedrooms and even music from the bar downstairs. It's Christmas Eve tomorrow. Lots of people are celebrating and are probably getting drunk. She needs to concentrate on her next piece of artwork and then get to bed. She doesn't feel sleepy though. She clears the cushions off the bed and puts her handbag on the bedside cupboard.

The towel falls from her as she bends over the bed. She flings it on the floor. It's a bit of a struggle writing on the duvet cover and excess pillows. When she's finished she admires her handiwork.

TO A LOAD OF B'S,

BASTARDS, aBUSERS, BUMS,

BRITISH BIGOTED BREXITEERS,

BOLLOCKS TO THE LOT OF YOU!

In full flow now, she grabs the towel and goes to the bathroom. She wipes the mirror glass with it and simply writes,

THE BBB WAS HERE!

She dumps the towel in the bath, brushes her teeth and gets into bed. She turns the telly back on, scrolls through the channels and settles on a wildlife programme. She turns the sound low so that it is purely soporific. She stares round her, at the duvet cover, at the mirrors. She turns the light off.

The strange noises are nothing compared to the strange feelings in Beth's brain. This is what I'm leaving behind, my mark of rebellion, of revenge, after 30 years of hard work and behaving myself in a most adult and responsible manner. She doesn't understand Gavin, she doesn't understand herself either. She doesn't understand why there had to be a referendum. Her whole life has been shaken up by it and altered for good. She can't cope with the whole state of affairs, the ones in her own life and the ones in the country. She simply wants calm, predictability, normal behaviour from people around her.

By midnight she turns the telly off and goes for a final pee. Her exhaustion overtakes her and she sleeps soundly until her alarm wakes her.

She makes a cup of coffee and sips it sitting up in bed. With the little sidelight on the graffiti is only visible on a semi-conscious spectrum; it's blurred, the lines of her writing appearing like strands of Christmas decorations, red ribbons on the inside of a room parcel. She has a weird feeling of self-satisfaction. Is this what sweet revenge tastes like, revenge for Sophia and her mates, revenge for the three million, revenge for herself?

She has a quick wash and packs her few belongings in her handbag. She pulls the duvet straight to make the writing as clear as daylight. It dawns on her that it won't be Peter Mezzo who will first clap his eyes on this grand state of affairs but one or other poorly paid chambermaid. She doubts if the chambermaid is Romanian. Those girls will have made sure that the agency won't send girls to this horrid place again. Or do such agencies care?

Beth is full of doubt about her actions. Too damn late now. She picks up her bag, takes the key and quietly tiptoes to reception, leaves the key and lets herself out. The hotel is in total silence as is the town. Not even the seagulls are awake. The first light is at least two hours away.

She gets in the car and drives away. Once out of town she turns her music on. Neil Diamond is still on repeat. 'And I can't even say why, leaving me lonely still'.

Beth pulls over in a lay-by. She gets her new phone and checks the time. Six o'clock. Fine. She dials her mother's number. It will be seven o'clock in Brussels. She'll be up.

Her mother answers cautiously. Beth puts her mind at rest immediately, reassures her that she has nothing to worry about. Finally, she drops the words she needs to say.

"Maman, je rentre chez moi!"

Beth ends the conversation immediately. She doesn't want to have to explain, she just wants to drive, drive east. She turns her music on loud. It's off repeat. The first track is the choicest one. Edith Piaf's gruff voice blares, 'Non, je ne regret rien' into the Welsh countryside.

"Farewell Wales," cries Beth, tears running freely down her cheeks. "I'm going home. The Brexiteers have won. I don't feel at home here anymore. Je suis Belgique!"

- o 0 o -